GHOSTS

Also by Ursula Perrin

Heart Failures
Unheard Music
Old Devotions

Harper & Row, Publishers, New York
Cambridge, Philadelphia, San Francisco, Washington
London, Mexico City, São Paulo, Singapore, Sydney

GHOSTS

URSULA PERRIN

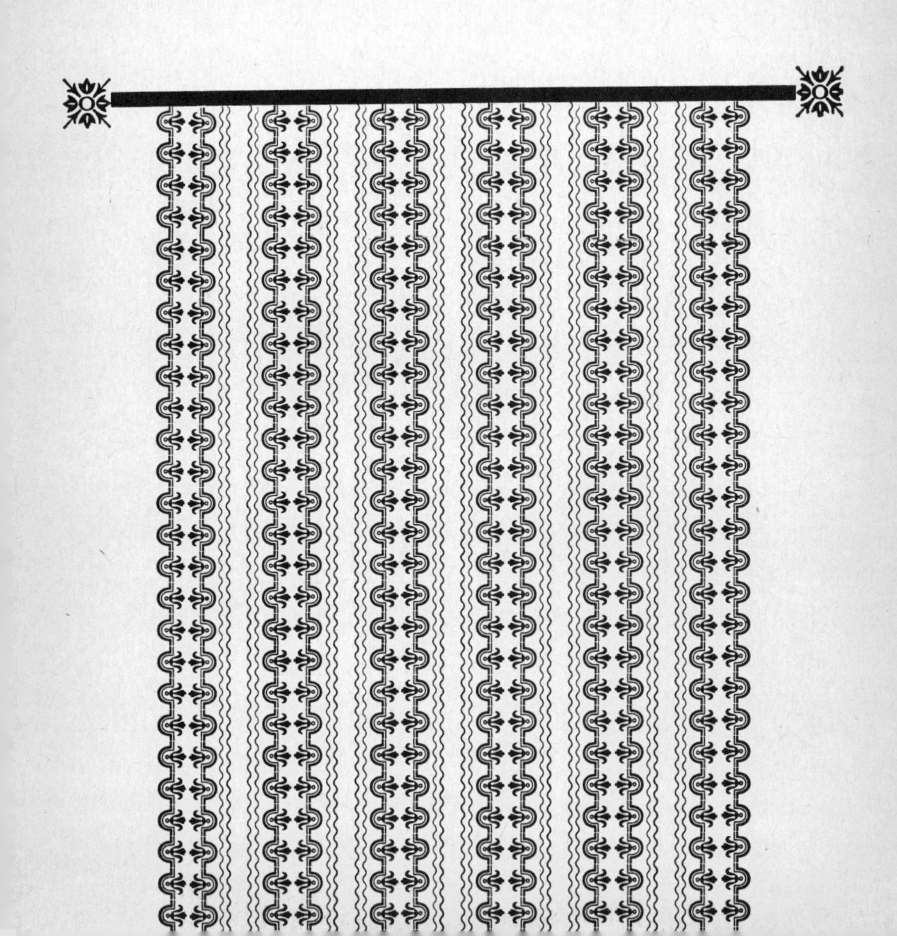

A condensation of this novel appeared in *Ladies' Home Journal*.

The epigraph from "A Process in the Weather of the Heart" is reprinted from Dylan Thomas's *Collected Poems*. Copyright 1953 by Dylan Thomas, © 1957 by New Directions. Reprinted by permission of the publishers, New Directions Publishing Corporation and J. M. Dent & Sons Ltd., and of the Literary Executors of the Dylan Thomas Estate.

A hardcover edition of this book was originally published in 1967 by Alfred A. Knopf, Inc. It is here reprinted by arrangement with the author.

 For information address Harper & Row, Publishers, Inc., 10 East 53rd Street, New York, N.Y. 10022. Published simultaneously in Canada by Fitzhenry & Whiteside Limited, Toronto.

First PERENNIAL LIBRARY edition published 1988.

Library of Congress Cataloging-in-Publication Data

Perrin, Ursula, 1935–
Ghosts.

Originally published: New York : Knopf, 1967.
I. Title.
[PS3566.E6944G4 1988] 813'.54 87-46163
ISBN 0-06-097162-2 (pbk.)

---

88 89 90 91 92 FG 10 9 8 7 6 5 4 3 2 1

FOR MARK

"A weather in the flesh and bone
Is damp and dry; the quick and dead
Move like two ghosts before the eye."

From "A Process in the Weather of the Heart" by Dylan Thomas

PART I

I

Nineteen forty-five. The rubble is still smoking and I am nearly ten on this warm Saturday late in April. President Roosevelt has died and our house, although split politically, wears an aspect of somnolent mourning. We move more slowly, talk softly, and my sister Sylvia's crying goes on as ever, adolescent tears washing away pubescence. She cries often. After every downpour her face emerges soft, gay as a washed garden. She cries today because she wants to go to a picnic with Bill Flipman and my mother has said, "No." Poor Syl, poor Sully, lazy, slow, beautiful as summer, she is fifteen and looks twenty and all her friends, she tells my mother, go out. She is tall with a solid, heavy-boned body, but long to the waist and small. Then her hips and legs take on a strange earthy heaviness as if she were rooted upward from the ground. She has skin the color of dark gold and lovely gold-flecked green eyes and her hair she wears straight down to her shoulders, turned under and hanging a little over one eye. The influence this year is Veronica Lake. "Don't you have a barette?" my mother asks. In my family, I am supposed to be smart and my brother Louis is smart. Sully is beautiful but not smart.

4

Outside my mother is mowing the lawn. The sound of it comes to me all warped by Sully's tears, and as I sit in my room, at my desk, the noise disturbs me, or rather the interstices do. These small suspensions hold each one the possibility of a summons—I know I should be in the garden too—but I go on with what I am doing, reading a book. I read a book every day trying to beat out Herbie Finster for the Sixth Grade Book Prize. I am ahead with 337 and Herbie with 322, though privately, I think he skips. The mower stops and I look up, the pencil I am fiddling with locked between my teeth, and wait.

"Syl-vee-uh."

I stare at the wall, waiting.

"SYL-vee-uh."

The crying stops. The springs of Sully's bed go "ping" and her door opens. She is barefoot, and in my mind I see the flash of her instep reflected in the glossy hall floor. She pads down to the porch at the end of the hall and I hear, "Yes?"

"Come down and help me now, you can cry some other day."

"I'm doing my Laa-tin, Mo-ther."

I snort to myself. Such stupidity, using this worn-out ploy.

"You can do your Latin tonight."

"Ellie isn't doing anything."

"Isn't she practicing?"

"No, she's reading, as usual."

"Then you both come out here. Tell Eleanor to put her book away, she'll ruin her eyes."

5

I take the pencil out of my mouth and get up and go out. At the head of the front stairs I wait for Sully, who is coming back down the hall, hair flying, and I stick out my tongue at her and she says, "Oh, go to," and slams her door in back of her. I go down the front stairs, through the second floor to the kitchen to get a peach, and then down the second-floor back stairs. Still, I am ahead of Sully who is probably combing her hair. Yes, here she comes with her hair combed and lipstick that she has put on and then, for my mother's sake, mostly wiped off. It is three o'clock and almost time for Bill Flipman to come by with the paper.

"Sully," my mother says, "you rake up and Eleanor, you loosen the dirt around the new petunias, will you please? I never saw two such girls for staying in the house. A beautiful day like this." And she goes whirring away, glued resolutely to the mower.

Watching my mother I feel guilty. She looks hot. At the end of the lawn she stops, lifts the neckline of her dress, and flaps it back and forth. There is a rosy flush in the area just above her bosom. The pepper and salt curls on her forehead are damp.

"Why don't you let me mow?" I ask.

"No, no, I'll do it. It's good for what's left of my figure." My mother doesn't really like to garden, but someone, she says, has to do it.

Our house doesn't have much of a garden, but what we have is a nuisance. If we were going to have a garden, Sully and I would rather have it with a house up on the Hill, where everybody else we know lives. We're the only kids we know who live downtown. We live in a big three-story yellow-brick house on the second-busiest downtown street in Clifton. Our house is separated by a driveway from the Elks Club on the east, and by another driveway from the Mohawkin Glove Factory (west). The Alhambra Movie is right around the corner on Hill and Main. The YMCA, where I swim on Thursdays (Ladies' Day), is across the street and we have always set our clocks by the large illuminated one that hangs over the Y's sidewalk. Our church, the First Presbyterian, is three blocks away, catty-corner from the public library. I don't mind it much downtown because we are pretty close to all these things, but Sully would like to be able to hang out at Charlie's, where the Hill crowd and Bill Flipman hang out.

"I wish I had your energy, Mother," Sully says. To rake the lawn she uses the same movement she does to comb her hair, long and languid.

"Maybe it'll come to you," my mother says, but breathlessly. She is stuck on a bump and tugs at the mower strenuously. The mower snaps, snarls, then leaps forward spitting a froth of grass, while my poor mother hangs on behind.

"Hey!" Sully says, scrambling. My mother stops just short of Sully's bare foot and laughs, and Sully laughs too. Then I see by the look that is crystallizing in my sister's eyes—hope glints there like sugar—that she is going to give it one more try. She looks up from under the gold waterfall of hair.

"Mother," she begins.

My mother's face, which a minute ago had been open

and laughing, now snaps shut. The deep crease between her eyes seals itself. "No," she says. "I explained to you, Sylvia, why you cannot go."

Sully's look is glazed, her eyes drop.

"Billie is a nice boy but you are too young to go out with those boys. If it were daytime I'd say all right, but no, not with those boys at night. All they do is drink out there anyhow."

"Oh!" Sully's eyes widen in despair. "They do *not,* where'd you ever hear *that?*" Worse and worse, where will it end? Soon they won't let her go to school.

"I know all about what goes on at the lake."

"The boys in Sully's class drink, Mother," I say righteously.

"You liar," Sully says hotly, "they do not. She's lying, Mother, honestly."

"Yesterday," I say, smug, "I saw Martin Vorhees and Peter Whitney go into Poole's Bar and Grill."

"Oh, really," my mother says, throwing up her hands, "do you think I care? They can swill like pigs, they'll all end up in the mill anyhow. Which is exactly why you girls shouldn't go out with them. Now, Sylvia, just forget it. Tonight we'll all go to the movies together."

"Oh!" Sully says. Her shoulders hunch, her eyes squeeze shut in pain. "I can't think of anything more ex-o-tic." And she walks rigidly toward the house.

Now my father arrives, stopping the exhausted Ford just short of catastrophe under the Elks' side-driveway porte-cochere. "Hello, gorgeous," he calls to Sully as he gets out, but she doesn't answer; her lower lip curls like a baby's, and she is going up to her room to cry some more. My father hauls his black bag out of the car and drags it, as if it were full of stones, to the steps of the porch. "Hi, gang," he says. "What's wrong with our beauteous daughter?" he asks my mother.

"You mean me, Daddy?" I ask, to tease.

"No," he says vaguely, and then, "Oh, hi, sport, I didn't see you down there. How's tricks?"

"Sully wants to go to a picnic with Bill Flipman," I say.

"Bill who?" my father says, and blinks. He is near-sighted and perhaps it is this that makes him seem so bewildered by the world beyond his large round lenses. Bill has delivered our evening paper for three years but my father still thinks of him as someone else, Henry or George, maybe.

"The paper boy, Fred," my mother says. "I told her no."

"He seems like a nice boy," my father says.

"He is a nice boy," my mother says. "The point is, he's eighteen and Sully's only just fifteen. There's a world of difference between ninth grade and twelfth. Those boys drink like fish. They were out at Rita Hammel's over the weekend and she told me that all Monday morning she kept finding beer bottles. Even in the beds, as well as"—she throws a careful look in my direction and goes on in a lowered voice—"other things." Other things! I keep my head bent close to the petunias but my ears lift as if by themselves. I make a mental note to report this to Sully.

"Poor Sylvia," my father says, now easing himself down on the steps. He does not quite sit on his seat but on the side of his leg, and I know he's had a hard day. "The trouble with Sully is, she's got the body of a woman and the brain of a pea."

"Shh," my mother says, frowning and looking up at the third floor where Sully is crying.

"Just fooling," my father says, extra loud. *Sotto voce* he says to my mother, "How'd we ever get one like that? You must have a hidden side to your family tree."

"She looks exactly like that picture of your mother," my mother states firmly. Now she begins to finish the raking Sully left and with short efficient strokes combs the lawn clean. Then she bends, scoops up all the clippings in her arms and dumps them into an empty bushelbasket, and then carries the loaded basket over to the trash barrel and dumps. This done, she walks up the steps past my father. At the door she kicks off her gardening shoes, grass-spattered Red Cross shoes with the toes cut out, and scuffs into a squash-sided pair of moccasins.

"When Louis gets home," my father says, "you won't have to do all that." He gets up slowly, lifts the bag, and without taking off his hat, only flicking it to the back of his head, follows my mother into the house. They disappear up the stairs, then as they reach the second-floor porch their heads reappear, and then they disappear again, and I finish around the petunias and go on to the baby marigolds, little bright stalks I love. I finish around the marigolds and dust off my hands and go quietly but not sneakily up the back stairs, through the second-floor porch, up to the third floor, and down the hall to my room. Sully has stopped crying—from the silence I gather she is sleeping. I start reading my book thinking 337 to 322, but then I think about Louis, and I get my V-mail folder and start writing him a letter, printing very small to save space.

My dear brother Louis,

I can't tell you how much we all miss you here, now that it's time to do the garden.

I want it to be funny and I sit and chew on the chewed end of the pen. I'd like to tell Louis how much we really all do miss him, how now that he is gone my father is stunned by all the women and has no one to play chess with. How there is no one now who knows how to tease Mother out of her depressions. How there is no one to shout Sully out of the third-floor bath and no one to play badminton with me in the glove factory driveway and no one for me to talk to, now that he is gone, at least not anyone who knows the names of almost all the birds, and many butterflies, and all the players in the American League; and late at night, when he thinks we are asleep, my father roams the house with a Seven-Up until my mother calls to him from the bedroom (Fred? Fred, for heaven's sake!), and how my mother does not play the piano, but often at night I see her sitting alone in the bedroom, in the dark, and she is just sitting there, in her chair next to the window, looking at the blacked-out windows of the Mohawkin; and how all of us, dear Louis, miss you so.

It's hot in my room so I take my letter out to the porch to

finish it. Downstairs, on the second-floor porch, I can hear my father saying, "I don't know, I might try rice today. And some peas, strained. All of this cheese is going to kill me sooner or later. This stuff I've been on, stuff Pfizer puts out, doesn't seem to be the thing. Maybe I ought to go down to Albany and see Everett. He knows a hell of a lot more than McMurray. When McMurray operates, it's little Jack Horner all over again."

My father, a general practitioner, hates surgeons, although he is always telling Louis that's what he ought to be. "Make the money," he says, "that's what counts, Louis. And the way to do it is, let them feel those scars. That's what they think they're paying for. You don't really have to know anything, just learn some anatomy and put your brains to bed. First-year medical school and the rest of your life is taken care of." Now he asks my mother if she will make him some tea and she says "Yes-yes-*yes*" although from her voice I can tell she's rooms away, in the bedroom. The doorbell rings. That Sully can get to phones and doors faster than anyone, even asleep, and looking up, I see her go streaking by.

"I'll get it," she yells.

I go downstairs too. Nasty girl that I am, I plan to wait on the first-floor landing to witness the denouement of the picnic affair. Slipping down the stairs, I expect to see Sully with one arm up, leaning on the inside of the screen door, and Bill leaning against her from the outside, their arms separated by cruel mesh. At the second floor I hear Sully's voice and I think, what a baby, she's crying right in front of

Bill. "Mo-o-ther," her voice wobbles. My mother runs out ahead of me on the stairs, wiping her hands on her apron, and now in back of me comes my father, and we all three stand on the stairs and look down. There is Sully, her face crumpled and scared, and there, on the other side of the screen, this kid I have never seen before with a telegram.

It was my mother who went down the stairs, moved Sully aside, and took the telegram from the boy (who wore, despite the warmth, his crimson silk-and-wool Clifton High School jacket). I went down the stairs and stood next to my mother, timidly and without touching her. Her eyes were gray, cold, frozen, gray. She tore open the telegram, read it, and then turned to go back up the stairs. As she did so, she passed the hall radiator and idly, as if she were putting down a book, laid the telegram upon it. My father, through all this, stood clinging with both hands to the bannister and he did not look at my mother as she passed. Then he came very carefully down the stairs, holding to the railing all the while, and picked up the telegram and read it. My mother had gone up into the bedroom and closed the door. He, now, like a blind man, stumbling a little and using his hands to help him, the telegram clutched in his fingers like a dirty flag, went into his office and shut the door. Sully was hunched into her corner, whimpering, and I went upstairs to my room.

I lay on my bed and shut my eyes. It seemed to me very important to figure things out, but I couldn't. My head felt clogged and dull, full of a rubbery mucus. It got dark and I slept. I couldn't cry, I was much too frightened, and about ten, feeling ashamed of my hunger, I went down to the kitchen and ate some bread. There was no light under the door of my parents' room and no sound. I went back upstairs. Sometime during the night my mother came in and sat for a while on my bed but I was afraid of her and pretended, by breathing slow and loud, to be asleep.

Our lives resumed at breakfast. When I went down to the kitchen my mother was making coffee and boiling eggs. I slid into my place with my head down. Sully was snuffling across from me and my mother, shoving an egg cup in front of her, said roughly, "Oh, stop it." My mother looked very tired. Her face sagged and in it only her eyes were hard, as if, overnight, all her strength had seeped from her flesh and become concentrated in those bright little chunks of ice. My father did not come upstairs until late afternoon. He had spent the night in his office and somehow, in these strange night-time surroundings, had broken his glasses. About four we heard him climb the stairs, very slowly, and he came into the living room with his hand against the wall. He looked at us with his dazed naked face and held up the glasses, showing us the crushed lens. His voice without the glasses was different, and wandered as if it too were blind.

"Look, Frieda," he said, in his high new voice, "see what I've done."

My mother was sitting in her chair, turning the pages of a magazine. She looked up at him and then down at the shiny page she was holding. "I see, Fred," she said, "you've broken your glasses."

And that was all. My father sat down and after a while

began to read, holding the book close up to his eyes. At five I heard a car stop and Sully went quietly down the stairs and the car door slammed. The motor did not start. I couldn't look at my parents. Is this all? I wanted to ask. Tell me, is it? Will everything be just the same?

I wanted them to tell me no, but it was quiet, terribly quiet. There was only the whirring tick of the shelf clock and the slip-slip-slip of the endlessly turning pages.

2

That summer everyone was kind to me because my brother had been killed in the war. At camp I learned to swim and found a friend, Sue. She had about a billion freckles and was the best swimmer in the intermediate unit.

> *When you get married and have some twins,*
> *Come to me for safety pins*

she wrote in my red leather Cheewonko album. On the last day we rode the camp bus together, down from the mountains into Twin Falls. There she took the train for Syracuse and I waited at the camp bus stop for my father. I waited an hour and a half, pretending to read, sitting on my duffel at the busy corner of Front Street and Arbutus, and all the while passers-by eyed me humorously, a fat ten-year-old, still in green camp shorts and chocolate-stained tee shirt. Then, furious, with the duffel dragging and my mother's scratched black suitcase bumping my heels, I caught a bus for Clifton, then found I had no money and had to be trusted, and had to stand the last thirty miles between a beery, burping fat man and a skinny office type whose spike heels kept throwing her off balance against me, against him.

16

Then in Clifton I was dumped again at the corner of Main and Hill with eight blocks to walk, the suitcase and duffel all the while bumping my heels.

At home I half pushed, half kicked the gear up the Mohawkin-side driveway to the back. My incompetent and thoughtless parents. Who else but me, I figured, would ever have to do this? I climbed the back stairs without starch enough even to yell, but Sully heard me and shouted down, "Who's that? Is that you, Eleanor?"

"Who were you expecting, Sylvia? Your paramour? Where is everybody?"

She was up on the third-floor porch. This porch had always been the children's and thus was unscreened and furnished with careless specimens: a splinty rocker, a wooden folding chair, the chaise so stiffened from exposure that hours after you left it flecks of its navy-blue skin still adhered to yours. Sully was lying on this chaise chewing gum and reading a copy of *Teen Love*. Her bare legs were brown and crossed and her foot moved in time to some music I did not hear.

"A fine welcome home," I said and flopped into the rocker. "I've just spent half my life getting here from Twin Falls."

She turned a page and went on looking at the magazine. "Daddy forgot. Mother's at the A&P. How are you, old girl?"

"Swell," I said moodily and then added, "I got my Swimmer's."

She snapped her gum. "Goody."

17

"*You* never got it."

"I never had all that fat to float on." She stared at me. "You look worse, by the way. What'd you do, get one of the girls to sell you her candy allowance?"

I was sensitive about my fat but couldn't think of anything acid to say to this because it was true; Mary Agnes Walton had sold me her Tuesday and Saturday after-lunch Snickers for fifteen cents apiece. So I got up and went to the door and she looked up again and said, "Gee, I'm sorry, Ellie. I'm getting to be a witch. Live around this house long enough and it'll do something to you." She threw the magazine down and sat up straight and started biting the cuticle of her right thumb. Her Veronica Lake spilled golden over the side of her face. "You don't *know,* you can't imagine what this summer's been like. It's been crazy. Mother gets up to clean at five A.M. and Daddy is up all night and sleeps all day. If it weren't for Bill I guess I'd be pretty near crazy too." She got up suddenly and moved her head, beckoning me to follow, and we went into the third-floor hall.

Like the porch, the third floor itself was mainly for the children. On the unheated side there was a large storage room, and on the heated side Louis's room (in front), and then the bathroom, and my room, and then, in the back, Sully's room. I'd always hated being in the middle. Sully had a window on the porch and could look right out into the top of the pear tree, and Louis had the front and the people and the cars, and there was I, in the middle between city and country, with nothing but a view of the glove factory's black tar roof. We passed Sully's room with its week's worth of tossed underpants and socks, and then my room, neat because I hadn't been there, and stopped at the closed door that was Louis's room. Sully lifted her head as if to listen, and I heard my heart pounding in my ears. She nodded slightly and opened the door. Suppose, I thought, it were all different? Or all exactly the same? But no, look: his bed, his desk, his green-leather chair. All there. Only everything closed up and dusty. Sunlight falling in long dusty beams through the windows. The air choked and sweet. Then, looking at his bookcase, I saw the books were gone. Sully went to the closet and opened the door. This, too, was empty.

"There," she said. "Now what do you think?"

"Where'd it all go?"

"She gave it all away."

"All of it?" I couldn't believe it. Not the microscope he had saved a year to buy and the bug books, beautiful, with their wide glossy pages and elegant lepidoptera, and durable beetles looking malevolent, shiny, as if fantastically camouflaged for war in a painted desert. Mushrooms, birds, history, the *Stargazer's Manual,* and *How To Win at Poker* had also occupied these shelves.

"All of it gone. She gave it to the Salvation Army and the Clifton public library. I thought she'd at least give Bill some of the clothes."

"Bill!" I said. "Why him?"

She blushed anyway. "Well, isn't it better for someone you know to have the things? I mean, if you're going to give it away to just anybody—"

19

I heard my mother come in downstairs and went coldly past my sister out of the room. Downstairs, in the kitchen, my mother was standing in her stocking feet lifting groceries out of a bag.

"Oh, Eleanor!" she said and put down a can of peaches to hug me. Her skin smelled of fresh-ground coffee. "I'm so sorry about today. I've been so worried. Daddy went off to Bordentown this morning before I could remind him and by the time I'd called the camp you were gone."

"Mother, did you really give all Louis's things away? I mean his butterfly books and the microscope?"

She turned her head and went back to lifting out groceries. Her face, which in full was relaxed and flushed with the late August heat, took on in profile a calm, etched look. Her nose was so handsome and straight, her chin so Germanically firm.

"Did you manage all right with the suitcase and duffel?"

I nodded yes, my throat full of tears.

"I couldn't think of what to do. Your father's so forgetful. To go off like that without a word. Just leaving me a note. It's a good thing you're such a sensible girl." She lifted out a five-pound sack of sugar and sugar grains skittered on the floor. "Oh, really!" she cried. "That's the third time I've gotten a torn bag there. Those boys are so careless, they don't give a hang. Just throw things on the shelves any old way. Daddy has the microscope and I saved the history books for you. I didn't think you cared about the bugs."

"What's Daddy doing with the microscope?" I asked.

Sully had come in and was leaning against the door

watching us. She laughed. "He thinks he's discovering the cure for cancer."

I supposed that Sully was being funny but my mother did not correct her, just went on emptying the other bag—probably the only woman in Clifton who would carry two large sacks of groceries home ten bocks. Then she said to Sully, "If you're going to the lake you'd better get started. Bill will probably be here soon."

Mondays through Fridays my father had evening office hours from seven to nine and my mother, who was a bad cook, claimed the six-thirty deadline as her reason. The truth, I think, was that she learned to dislike cooking at Schlegel's. Before she married my father she worked for four years as a cashier in her uncle's delicatessen-restaurant, in a densely German part of New York City. My mother was born in Germany and came to this country with her father, brother, and sister (her mother already dead) when she was five. It was difficult. My grandfather, in the picture I have of him, is a straight-featured, beardless man, handsome, but looking as my mother says he was. Taciturn. A dreamer, tinkerer, inventor of small gadgets, he smoked a pipe and liked to eat apples in the evening. He invented an automatic apple corer and, before such things were thought of, an electric shaver. But no one was interested. He had no luck. Instead, small jobs were found for him. He worked at repairing watches but thought this beneath him. He sold carpets but found he had no business instincts—neither that need for money, strong as physical desire, nor love of the business game. In Germany he had been a postal inspector and wore a uniform. One sleety February day he was struck by an electric trolley at the corner of Broadway and Fourteenth Street, Manhattan. With the small amount of money he'd left, my mother's brother went to college and medical school. She worked at the cash register where all day long she bonged out change for toothpick-chewing gents and in between read soberly, ever hopefully, from Compton's Classics. She had wanted to study—but what? She had wanted to be something—but what?

Tonight she is out on the second-floor porch reading when I come down from my room.

"Are we going to eat sometime?" I ask plaintively.

She looks startled and says, "Is it that time already?"

"It's after six," I say, although it is in fact only two past.

She sighs and lays the book she is reading face down on the floor and stands up. I sit down on the chair she's been sitting in and pick up the book and for want of something to do begin reading where she's stopped. She stands in the doorway with a troubled look.

"What would you like for dinner?"

"How do I know?" I say. "You went shopping."

"Eggs?" she suggests hopefully and then, her face clearing, says, "That's right! I'd forgotten about the pork chops." She goes into the kitchen and begins searching the kitchen cupboard for cooking utensils. Generally, they are all tangled together on the bottom shelf—eggbeaters with only one beater, bent stirring spoons, knives that don't cut anything except fingers. All of the pot covers have holes where the handles are supposed to be, and her only frying pan has the toes-up profile of a worn shoe. She hasn't bought anything for the kitchen in fifteen years and now she scrambles through this junkyard of culinary equipment, looking for something. Through the clatter and bang, she tells me about my father's new diet.

"Ground carrots," she says, "and applesauce. No milk, bread, butter, eggs, meat, or fish. No wheat or wheat products. Cancer. They're cancer-producing agents." She has found what she is looking for, the long cooking fork with tines that separate like antennae, and she beats this into her palm as she talks.

"Then I asked him, what if you do get cancer, we all have to go sometime. Do you want to live forever? And do you know what he said to that? Yes. Yes! Can you imagine? Not for me, I said. I don't want to go on and on, creeping around half blind and deaf, with palsy and God knows what, and living on my children. Then he asked me, if I didn't care, wasn't I interested in saving other people's lives."

"What did you say then?" I asked her, although I am embarrassed by this. I feel, after all, my father is more her problem than mine.

"I said there were too many people in the world already and what for?"

This puzzles me. What does she mean, what for? I am about to ask but the grease, which has been sizzling in the pan, gets very excited, and she jumps to turn down the gas, and the waiting-room bell rings, and my mother goes "Tsch," looks at the clock, unwraps her apron, and with fork still in hand goes out toward the front stairs to welcome the first of the evening's patients. My father arrives at eight, carrying seven books. His carrots and applesauce (mixed) have long since cooled on the kitchen table and two of thc patients have gone home.

What I like to do, the first day I'm back from camp, is to walk around looking at the new magazines and books. A whole summer's pulpy harvest! Then, sated with *Life* and *Collier's,* and the *Reader's Digest,* I tour the rooms. They always look better after two months' absence, comfortable instead of wartime worn. The fade of the blue-flowered chintz drapes is soft, the balding spot on the dining-room rug familiar, the creak of the plush maroon chairs, the sag of the green sofa cushions, all these things are homey, dear. I am reassured. Despite a new glass ashtray, nothing much is different after all.

For one reason or another I don't get around to my parents' bedroom until just before I go to bed. It looks pleasantly neat to me, although I'm not sure why. My mother is sitting at the writing table with a stack of bills, and when I come in she moves her left hand slightly, as if to cover them.

"Going to bed?" she says. "It's getting late."

"In a while," I say. "What are you doing?"

"Going through some bills." I have never seen her do this before. My father always had certain evenings in the month when he would sigh and mumble and squint and blot into the marblized account book my mother now has open before her.

"Why are you doing that?" I ask. She is in the middle of a column of figures, her lips move, her pencil hops lightly, and when I ask this she sighs and puts the pencil down. She rubs her eyes with her fingertips and yawns.

"Because," she says. "Someone has to do it." Then she picks up the pencil again and the pencil hops toward her this time, from the top of the column. I wander around the room and stop to admire the objects on the bureau. I hold and stroke the little porcelain goose, loving with my fingers its smooth egg-shaped body and the sudden adjustment my fingers have to make, from placid oval to attenuated angry neck. At camp I tried to make a similar thing out of clay but in rolling the stuff between my palms could never get this same slender distention. I put the goose down and observe that my father's hairbrushes are gone. My mother has cleaning days during which every unused object disappears, and I attribute the loss of the brushes to this. I go over to the double bed with its bookcase headboard, to see what the Book of the Month has sent us this summer. The bookcase headboard looks unusually tidy, and then it occurs to me that the year's supply of the *Journal of the AMA* has been cleared away, and so has the rusty tole tray on which my father kept a supply of medicines, ten or twelve bottles he could not get through the night without. His ashtray, a large brown beanbag with a copper inset, has been replaced by a bottle of Dr. Scholl's.

"Gee," I say, lifting up the Scholl's to smell it (I have a friend, Patty Byers, who knocks herself out by smelling fingernail polish), "you really have been cleaning, haven't you?"

"What?" my mother says, frowning and lifting her head.

"I mean all Daddy's stuff being gone."

In the glow of the desk lamp her face looks pink, then shifts to a ruddier color. "Daddy is sleeping downstairs now," she says. "In the office."

"He is?" I ask. "What for?" The Scholl's doesn't seem to have the same magical properties as Revlon, and I screw on the cap and look at her. She puzzles me. Why is she fidgeting?

"He's been so sick this summer," she says. "He's up all night prowling and he keeps me awake. I can't sleep all morning the way he does. Besides," she says, shuffling the bills together, "when he's not in the bathroom, he likes to read. So you really liked camp this summer?"

"Yeah," I say. "It was all right."

She snaps the account book shut. "I'm glad you enjoyed it," she says, "because it cost a lot of money."

"Then why do I have to go?" I say. "I'd rather stay home anyhow."

"Because if you didn't go to camp you'd never get out of doors into the sun. You'd sit on that porch and read the summer away. Do you know why they call people who read too much bookworms? Because eventually their skins turn all white and pasty."

"Relax, Mother," I say. "You don't have to fuss over me. You've got my beautiful sister Sully."

"That's right," my mother says, "I do that."

"I'd rather be pretty than smart," I say gloomily, prodding to get her praise.

"All I ask is that you look healthy. Beauty doesn't last," she reminds me sternly.

"The bloom on the flower, Is blitzed in an hour" I quote to her from my Cheewonko album.

"Exactly," she says. "Now go to bed. It's late." She sees that I have a book of hers hidden under my arm and says, "If you stay up too long reading, you'll ruin your eyes." Then smiles at me, hugs me, and gives me a small push toward the door.

But I plan to read a long time tonight. The trouble with camp is that there is never any time to read. The counselors are busy getting you to bed at nine so that they can sit in their tents and smoke and talk about their boyfriends, and this year I had a snotty girl in my tent who reported me for reading under the blankets with a flashlight. Nobody liked this girl, which was nice for me since last year it was me nobody liked. Last year I didn't get along at camp at all, but this year I made an adjustment in that I didn't complain. I did all the stupid things, even the senseless folk dancing. Tra-lalalala! This is called being a Stoic, which I read about last spring. What bothers me is that it seems cowardly. I mean, if there is something you don't like and you go along with it, isn't that wrong? According to my father that is what is wrong with the German people, although I think he brings this up when he wants to irritate my mother.

Anyway, it's nice to be home. Probably the best reason for going to camp is that it makes you appreciate home. After not reading for so long, and eating only three times a day, it seems a unique and particular freedom to be able to do both tonight after ten o'clock. I get a sour green apple from the kitchen and take it up to my room, putting it on the book under the table lamp. I get a clean pair of pajamas from the drawer of my bureau and it is very nice to have a clean dry pair—nothing accumulates under canvas like moisture. For a month everything I'd put on was clammy. The bed, my old iron friend, groans as I get on it and I pull up the dry, rustling sheet and open the book and bite into the apple. The sounds of the house settling down surround me. My mother goes down the stairs to lock the door, I hear a racket in the pipes, and the sound of my father's slippers. Surprisingly, they come all the way up to the third floor and go as far as the storage-room door. I read for a while, but the book is bad, and I get up and go down the hall and knock on the door.

"Yes," my father says.

"It's Ellie, Daddy," I say.

My father opens the door and peers out at me as if he didn't know whom to expect. "Oh, Eleanor," he says, "I thought you were asleep." He has on his old striped terry-cloth beach robe and blue-and-white striped pajamas, and between his fingers is a cigarette with a long ash. He doesn't really smoke cigarettes, he just lights them.

"What are you doing up here?" I ask, staring over his shoulder.

"This is my—uh—laboratory," he says. "I'm culturing several different kinds of—uh—fungi, you see, and they get in the way downstairs. This is a very convenient place, really. I can keep all the books and papers on my work separate from the things down in the office."

I walk around the room looking at the laboratory. It certainly does look odd. He has put round glass dishes with a jelly in them on the old wobble-legged wooden table, and things are growing on these jellies. He has taken over the yellow-pine roll-top desk, furnishing it with a lamp and his beanbag ashtray and a pile of handwritten notes and a typed list of books, and all over the room, on the large leprous green velvet armchair, and on top of the three-foot-tall pile of *National Geographics* and on the large painted wooden chest that holds old toys, and on the Heinz Tomato Soup cartons labeled Clothes—summer, Clothes—winter, there are books and medical journals and pamphlets, all spiny with slips of paper bookmarks. As I walk around examining the jellies, my father walks behind me, explaining what they are. Every so often he picks up one of his books and reads a paragraph to me from it, then slams the book shut on its mark with a satisfied look. From what I understand, he is catching cancer bugs out of the air onto the jelly and growing them. Or something.

"Well, that's real interesting," I say.

"Really," he says.

"Huh?"

"*Really* interesting," he says. "Don't say real interesting, it makes you sound like a Clifton hick. One thing about your mother, she may never have gone to college but she uses correct English."

"Do you think it's important?" I ask.

"Certainly," he says, "it's very important."

"Why?"

He considers this a moment and then says, "Because it's important to try to do things well. Aside from that, it's not important."

I don't think that's the reason my mother speaks carefully; it's because she doesn't like to sound uneducated, although she keeps telling us she is. My father sits down in the precarious swivel chair in front of the desk and drops his cigarette into the ashtray. He begins reading and I say, to bring the conversation back to me, "Daddy, do you think I should get married or go to college?"

He looks up and blinks. "I didn't know the question had come up."

"I've just been thinking about it lately, just this summer. I can't figure out what I want to be, and I figure if I don't know there's no point in going."

He turns a page. "I suppose that's true," he says.

"Though I don't know. Patty Byer's sister Margaret says it's the only thing to do because what else is there after high school? Anyway, I can't figure out what I'd like to be because this year I liked science best but I didn't like it last year."

"What other subjects do you like?"

This is a difficult question. It seems to me I like almost everything except arithmetic. I like especially science, history, and English, that is, the reading part of English, not the boring grammar. I can't think of an adequate, impressive answer to my father's question and so, partly because it's definite and partly to flatter his interest (which seems to have wandered again), I say, "I think I'd like to be a doctor."

But his reaction is disappointing. "A doctor, eh," he says, "well, we'll see. Isn't it time for you to go to bed?"

"Don't you believe in education for women?" I ask him.

"Of course I do," he says.

"Grandfather Schlegel didn't, did he?"

"Your Grandfather Schlegel was a Nineteenth-Century German. Go along now, Eleanor, I've got some work to do here." He frowns down at the page and says "ahh" at it, and begins looking through the papers for his pen, and then starts scribbling in his tiny unreadable scrawl. I feel sorry for him sitting there. The light in the room is so stark and he so small and pale and his gray hair looks dusty. He seems very old to me.

"Night, Daddy," I say at the door and after a minute, with the pen scratching away, he says, "Good night," and I close the door and go back to my own room.

. . . . .

31

I have read about a quarter of the book when Sully knocks.

"Entrez," I say. She comes in in a pair of shortie pajamas. They are pale blue with lace around the panty leg and around the collar. I know Mother didn't buy them; she buys all our nightwear directly from some factory in Pennsylvania. "Wow," I comment. "Where'd you get them?"

"Marianne," she says. Marianne is Bill's older sister who works in Penney's Department Store. "They were on sale so she bought them but they're too small for her." Sully sits on my bed and puts one leg up and starts examining her foot. "It's positively weird," she says, wriggling her toes, "they're getting all hairy, I don't know why."

"It's a disease," I say. "Will you kindly get them out of my face?"

She crosses her legs and speculatively scratches her kneecap and then stretches both of her legs out in front of her and yawns. "I wish I didn't have such fat thighs. What are you reading? Oh, that. I read that."

"You?" I snicker.

"Not all of it," she says. "Just the interesting parts toward the end. The middle is kind of boring. Anyway, you know what old T.R. said." In her ninth-grade English class they read an essay of T. Roosevelt's on it being better to live life than read about it, and she actually believes this. As if you weren't alive when you read. I make a noise in my throat and she lifts her head and gives me a wise big-sister look. "You know what?"

"No, what?"

"You're going to have trouble in junior high school because you have to be so darn smart all the time. It's all right to be bright, but do you have to let everyone know? I'll bet you're a real schnook in class, waving your little mitt in everyone's face."

"Boy, are you jealous."

"Jealous! What of? Your little sixth-grade marks? Wait till you hit Latin, kiddo, *then* talk. Listen, I'm not saying this to be mean. I'm just telling you for your own good. Boys hate girl grinds. The way to get ahead at JHS is, be friendly. Smile at everyone, even the creeps, only don't smile at them too hard. I mean, you don't want to get stuck. And maybe Mother'll let you cut off those icky braids."

"I like my braids," I say, though I don't.

"I'll bet she lets you wear lipstick before you're twelve. You wait. I was the guinea pig, now you get the benefits." She gives me more advice on skin and clothes and I listen because, after all, she has done well, was the only ninth-grade cheer leader and class secretary and went out with a basketball star. But after a while, I get a little restless. I have read all this elsewhere anyway, absorbing into my bloodstream I guess thousands of magazine words on how to be beautiful and popular. Staring at her thighs, I notice that the lace on the shorties does look tight, and scanning upward, see there is a hard lump obvious between the plummeting, unbraced softness of her breasts. I lean forward, pointing.

"What's that?" I say.

"What?" she says, as if she hadn't quite heard, but her hand goes nervously to this lump.

"That."

She shrugs, then reaches inside the nightie collar and hauls the thing up by its chain. It is a large gold ring, a CHS ring with the slab of garnet in the front, and I reach forward and grab it. "W.F. '45" is engraved on the inside of the band. It seems strange to me, this ring so lately on Bill's large hand now warm from my sister's skin. I let the ring drop and she tucks it back inside the lace-edged collar.

"I only wear it to bed," she says. "Don't tell Mother, all right?"

"She'd have a fit," I say.

"She has a fit whatever I do," Sully says.

"She just wants you to do well at school."

"I know it, Eleanor, but I can't. I mean, not the way she wants. Gee, I do better than lots of girls. I know I'm no genius but she acts as if I'm a moron. I mean, what good is all this Latin and stuff going to do me? And honestly, it's so boring. Wait till you have to do it, you'll see how boring it is. Gosh, I'm glad you're home though. When you're home she doesn't pick on me so much. You know what? She's been talking all summer about sending me away to school." She looks around the room—the walls have ears—and then bends her head close to mine. "Bill says if she does, we'll elope."

"You wouldn't," I say, sitting up straight.

"I would too, I'd to it tomorrow. What's the use of my dragging around CHS? I mean, Bill's got a good job now and when he finishes night school he'll get a better one. And all I want to do is get married."

34

"Oh, Sully," I say, "you don't mean that. There's so much else to do first. Don't you want to have a job and travel and meet people?"

She lifts her shoulders elegantly, then scoops her hands under her hair, letting it fall in a shower through her fingers. "You see, Eleanor, after we're married we probably will go to California. Bill says Clifton's got no future. He says now that the war's over, they'll start laying men off left and right. Anyway, I think I'd like it out there, it's so sunny and interesting."

Before she goes back to her room she turns at the door. "Gee, Ellie, I'm sorry I said that about your being fat. Actually, I think you've got potential. I mean, if you ever lose any weight you'll be a real cute girl."

"Really," I say.

"Huh?" she says.

"Skip it," I say.

"Well," she smiles at me, actually smiles, "good night, pest, sleep tight."

"Night," I say and she closes the door. My father's slippers go slip-slap down the hall and I hear Sully's heave upon the springs. Now it is all quiet and familiar and I snap off my light and turn on my side. At camp I was always the last asleep, lying on my cot listening drowsily to the varied fugal breathings of my tent mates, and just outside the fastened-down canvas, in the thick woodsy blackness, the night-time music of chirps, cheeps, buzzings, whines, and far-off howls. Here it is very quiet. At camp I would, last thing before sleeping, think of my brother Louis, remembering him as if lighting a candle, afraid that waking some bright morning my memory of him would be blank as the August sky. But here, in this quiet, it is hard to think. This quiet troubles me, it seems so heavy. It begins at his closed-up room and floats in a large damp cloud and descends the stairs. It touches my mother in her rocklike sleep and my father brushes it away as he scribbles and even Sully in her sleep moans as she feels its breath. And I am frightened and I turn under my sheet and wish, heart pounding, for the daylight.

3

Very early, from the kitchen, I hear my mother opening and closing the refrigerator door. Perhaps the June light has awakened her (at six the sun already steep and pushy against the shade), or nervousness because of the wedding, or both. It seems to me, anyway, that she's been up for hours. But I, despite the day's early gloriousness, feel heavy and dull, oppressed with my sister's sorrows, which are more mine than hers. Under the thin batiste of her wedding dress she will be three months pregnant.

My mother slams the refrigerator door extra hard and jostled forward by the vibration I sit up. I swing my legs over the bed, such fat legs, I think, and unbutton my pajama top and reach down for my bra which I'd dropped handily on the floor the night before. I stand up and kick off my bottoms—they fly up, then down, landing in a disgruntled heap at my feet. Ugly pajamas, I will all my life hate blue-and-white stripes, and I give them an extra little kick and then notice the small brown blot at the crotch. I pick up the things and inspect them closely, worrying. The day before, I fell forward riding John Ritchie's bike and this leakage seems to be the result. At least this type of rupture was what Patty Byers had warned me about. Now what will my future husband—that tall, rich, faceless man—think? Of course it could be a hemorrhage. I imagine a blasted vein, my blood spurting, then seeping down, down, down from my brain, squinched through my heart and out. I feel dizzy. I fold the pajamas so the stain doesn't show and then I think, "Oh no. It can't be that. Not today."

I put on the bottoms again, pulling them up tight around my waist and doubling the elastic band over, and go out to knock on Sully's door. At this moment my mother is coming up the stairs, walking carefully under unfamiliar hair. Usually, her gray hair is brushed back and pinned at the sides. For this occasion it has been dipped in a twilight violet and so tightly crimped it looks friable, as if the simple tap of a spoon would crumble it.

"Don't wake up Sully yet, Eleanor," my mother says. "Let her sleep."

I know I should ask my mother about my problem but I'd rather ask Sully. I look at her, confused.

"What's the matter?" my mother asks, knocking at the storage-room door.

"I—don't know," I say.

Her hand lifts to knock again. "Do you feel sick?"

I nod, and she says, "Well you can't get sick today, we don't have time. Do you have a stomach ache?" Her voice is a vexed echo out of my childhood—she used this same accusing tone when I was small. She never believed in my illnesses and now comes over and lays her warm, rough hand on my forehead. "You *feel* all right."

I blush slowly because I see I'm going to have to spell it out for her. "I think I've got the curse," I mutter, turning my head away from her hand.

"What?" she asks, frowning.

"I'm m-m-menstruating," I say. The difficult word feels thick and clots on my tongue. I feel hot all over.

"Oh, no," she says, shocked.

"I think so," I say.

My father opens his door and looks brightly at us, his hand clutching his pajamas because his strings always break. "Good morning, good morning," he says. "Is the bride asleep?"

My mother looks at him with her mouth open and I think, she's going to tell him right here, but she doesn't, she says, "Fred, will you please get yourself dressed? I don't know what time Herman's coming but it would be nice if we were all out of bed."

"I didn't know Herman was coming," my father says, although I distinctly remember my mother telling him two days ago. My mother's mouth pulls tight, she puts her hard hand on my shoulder and guides me back to my room.

"Sit down," she commands and disappears.

I am afraid to sit and instead stand, leaning against my desk. I am both frightened and excited by my condition. Of my friends, I am the last to start, a reward for being the youngest eighth-grade girl. They have told me, though, how to obtain materials inconspicuously: I am to go all the way down Main Street to Penney's Department Store. This store's interior is dim and brown, the floorboards creak, and its smell is the slightly acid one of cheap yard goods. Except for a few farm wives (who in timid pairs, like nuns, whisper and paw the flannels) it is usually empty. There I must go past a table full of stockings, past slinky lingerie, and glitter jewelry, and dusty notions, to the very back counter. Drugs. The stuff I want is prewrapped and ready to travel. The hard part is going home. This inconspicuous powder-blue prewrapping has become easy to identify and so the route has to be circuitous, to avoid meeting any of the boys I know. What's easier: to order it and have it delivered, but then, what about the delivery boy, Pinkie Cameron, who is in my Sunday School? Still, it will be interesting to call Patty and tell her in the code that I had to go to the Post Office for Stamps. Of course, on the other hand, I won't be able to swim now on all the Y's Ladies' Days, which leaves only three a month, and I will probably have to miss gym class and everyone will know why, and at night, when I walk home from Patty's house, I will no longer feel safe. And who wanted to have babies anyway?

"Everything happens at once," my mother says, coming back into the room. She extracts from the pocket of her housedress a sanitary napkin discreetly folded and a new packaged sanitary belt. "I don't know why Nature has to start things so soon. Such a nuisance." She puts the articles on my bureau and then sits suddenly, with a small sigh, on the edge of my bed. "How do you feel?" she asks. Without waiting for my answer she says, "You may have a little trouble. I always had a few aches and pains until I had children. That seemed to make everything go easier. The first time, I was your age and no one had told me anything. I didn't really have any one to talk to. My mother and sister were dead, my aunt was—well, I never could talk to that woman—and I didn't have any close friends. Finally, one of the girls in my class in school found me crying in the toilet. She explained it all." My mother smiled, in a girlish way that showed her crooked teeth. "She was my first real friend and for years she teased me, laughing at my stupidity."

"Where is she now?" I ask, curious because my mother seems to have so few friends.

"She's the lady who lives in Ohio, the one who always remembers your birthdays. Do you think you'll be all right?"

I nod, and my mother stands up. "You're a sensible girl and I guess you know all about things anyway." Then she smiles and dusts my cheek with her hand. "But you're still such a little girl."

I squirm. "I'm a horse," I say.

"Oh, nonsense," she says briskly and goes to the door. "When you get dressed you'd better wake up your sister or she'll sleep through the wedding." The doorbell jingles, making my mother jump. "No, you'd better get her up right now before that thing drives me crazy. I can't get this house clean and answer the door at the same time," and with an angry look she dives down the stairs, her moccasins burning a slap on every step.

By noontime, when Sully appeared in her robe and curlers and my father came out of the bathroom, shaven, bathed, and smelling strongly of Old Spice ("You'd think he was the bride," my mother commented bitterly), the housework was done. Chairs and side tables had been pushed into odd corners to make the ajoining living and dining rooms one. The dining-room table had been stretched into an incredible length, and covered with my mother's real Belgian lace tablecloth and set with silver cake forks. Flowers began to arrive. Delivery boys came with presents. The telephone kept ringing for Sully. She was the first of her friends to be married and they called to ask if she were nervous. At one o'clock my mother was still in moccasins and her hair had begun to melt around the edges. Whenever she heard a car she ran to the window, thinking it was Herman. At one-thirty she went upstairs to dress, and I followed.

In her room, that chaos, I found Sully sitting on the bed, filing her nails. The bed was strewn with clothes, her rocking chair held a tangled pile of shoes, on the dressing table was a clutter of bottles, jars, beads, bangles, pearls, and powder puffs, and out of this, rising like Fujiyama, a silver mountain of metal curlers, intricately stacked. Everything seemed about to slide into motion. In this near-flux of flimsy things Sully was a fixed vertical, entirely calm. She still wore curlers but had progressed from the pajamas into a stiff petticoat and a white lace merry widow that pinched in her waist and raised her breasts into a new, marital fullness.

"Going somewhere?" I asked.

"It could be," she said, looking up. "Congratulations, by the way, lucky girl-child."

"What for? Oh *that*. Thanks, I guess. I could have picked a better time."

"It always happens that way, when you don't want it. Feel okay?"

"Sure. I guess I had some cramps before." I went in and sat on the floor next to her, toeing away a crushed red skirt to do so. Her cheer-leading skirt, I saw. This year she would have been captain.

"Want that?" she asked.

"What, your skirt?"

"Uh-huh. I won't need it anymore."

"I never will, either. Besides, it wouldn't fit me."

"It might in a year or two. Take the sweater, anyway." She dug into the pile behind her on the bed and brought up the white turtleneck.

"Well gee, okay. Thanks."

"You're welcome. Want that girdle too?"

"Which one? This pink thing?"

"Yeah, now that you're so mature. It won't fit me in a couple of weeks, I know." Discreetly, I glanced at her middle, but there was no bulge at all. Perhaps it wasn't true, a story cooked up to get out of senior year. I couldn't imagine her having a baby.

"Sully?"

"Mmm?"

"Do you feel different now?"

"You mean because of the baby? Sure, slightly sick most of the time."

"Oh. Is that all?"

She stopped her filing to think. "Yes. It's hard to believe it's happening. I guess once I start getting bigger I'll believe it. Marianne says when you feel it kick you know you've got something. That's about the fifth month."

"Honestly? Would you write me when it does?"

"Are you kidding? If you're so curious go have your own." But she said this good-humoredly, with a poke of her bare painted toes into my side.

"Sully? You know about me, today? I feel so funny, as if everyone can see right through everything."

"Wear the girdle. It'll make you feel more secure."

"Don't you wonder what boys think about it? I mean men? These creeps in the eighth grade say such awful things. I'd feel awful if the man I married minded it."

"I don't think they mind. I don't think Bill ever did."

"You mean he knew when you were?"

She buzzed the emery board across her nails, blew on them, and scrubbed them on her knee. "Well, sure. We're getting married, after all. Your husband's supposed to know all that kind of thing. You want to tell him."

"You do? What for?"

"Oh, heavens, Ellie, I don't know," she said and flipped the file into an empty suitcase that stood, jaws propped, at the foot of the bed. Her abrupt dismissal of my quest made her seem suddenly older. The door she had closed shut off a room she shared with someone she would not betray, not even for me. I was awed. For the first time I saw her changed, growing Buddhalike, wise and serene, with the embryo folded (a kernel of truth) inside her.

"I'm sorry, Sully," I said. "You know something. You won't believe this, but I wish you weren't going so far away."

"I'll bet you can't wait till I go. You're dying to have this room."

"No, I'm going to keep my little hole, I'm used to it. Anyway, the closet's bigger."

"I'll miss it here," she said, "but Bill's right, Clifton's got no potential and they're laying off more men every month. Bill says he thinks Houghton's is going to close down anyhow. They'll all move South."

"That's crazy, they wouldn't leave the buildings and all," I said.

"Bill says labor's cheaper in the South and taxes and, boy, there isn't going to be much work around here in a couple of years. Anyway, Bill wants to get a different kind of job. You can't get ahead in the mill."

"California's so far," I said again. It wasn't so much California as the whole long trip into marriage that seemed distant, and the snug clutch of the Kotex belt at my loins didn't seem to take me any closer to it. I had somehow thought that when my time came my fat would mold itself into a woman's body and that I would know what a woman ought to know. Instead, I felt heavier and messy and like crying.

Sully stood up. "I guess I'd better pack," she said. Grandly, like a priestess performing a rite before the revels, she scooped a pile of stuff from the bed and let it fall, blessed, into the suitcase. I went back to my room to dress. By the time I had finished, my Uncle Herman was just coming up the stairs.

. . . . .

He marched upward in a general rumble of noise. He had never before been to Clifton, he was saying, and would not come again. He was being frank. He pronounced this harshly—"frrankk"—and the loudness of him, like a great breaking wave, over-rode my father's mild reply. He was ten, five years older than my mother, when the Schlegel family came from Germany, and his voice had retained a rough Germanic grit that my mother had, years ago, scoured away. He came through the door followed by my father, his wife, and then his sons, my cousins, Ted and Henry. He wore a dark plaid jacket and a red- and blue-striped bow tie, strange attire for a wedding, I thought, but he looked very clean. His crisp white hair was neat and trim, his skin clear and pink, and his slightly protuberant blue eyes looked freshly rinsed. When he hugged me, I smelled soap. His wife, Aunt Nesta, was small, fussy in a veiled hat and black silk dress splotched with roses. Her tiny feet were pushed into high-heeled open-toed shoes. She seemed inclined perilously forward, and when she kissed me my impulse was to lean back lest she fall. My mother said, "My, haven't the boys gotten tall," and Herman, in return, threw his arm around my neck.

"Hey, hasn't this kid grown?" he wanted to know. "What do you say, Ted, I'll bet you don't remember your cousin Eleanor as big as this." Ted grinned and Henry, his younger brother, snickered. I blushed and did not know where to look, gawky, stumbling, yoked under the awkward burden of my uncle's arm. The trouble was, I felt immense. The blue cotton dress I was wearing had been terrifically starched so that it swung out around me on all sides. I felt trapped by it, the dumb clapper of a large concrete bell. Tongue-tied, I looked up at my mother.

"Come," she said severely. "Let's all go out to the porch where it's cool."

Obediently, I followed my mother's mauve silk and we marched single file out of the living room, through the dining room, through the hall, into the kitchen. Behind me, my cousin Henry said, "Say, this town is really a dump. How do you stand it?"

"We like it," I said clearly. "It's in a very historical region."

"Yeah?" Henry said. "History of what?" and nearly fell off the step from the kitchen onto the porch. Ted laughed. We arranged ourselves on the furniture. Aunt Nesta of course took the chaise (the good, second-floor chaise, covered with cabbage roses, where she made a hyperbole of pattern, rose on rose), put her feet up, crossed her ankles, and began rooting in the enormous patent bag until she came up with cigarettes and a little ivory holder. My uncle had the other comfortable place to sit, a canvas-covered deck chair. My mother sat on a wooden folding chair, my father took the hassock, the boys sat on the porch stairs. Everyone lit cigarettes, even my mother, who held the cigarette at an odd angle behind her head, as if she expected it to go off. The boys were veiled by their own blue cloud of smoke. My uncle smoked a cigar.

"Gott damn it, Fred," he boomed at my father, who jumped, "what do you want to stick out here in this little town for?"

My father, perplexed, was trying to find and stamp upon the cigarette he had dropped on the straw rug. "Why—uh—it's not such a bad little town," he said, straining up sideways at my uncle and at the same time letting his fingertips scan the floor. "I was born here, you know. It's very nice country."

"The people here are lovely," my mother said.

"Geez, I don't understand it," my uncle said. "You leave a big booming place like New York. These past years I've made so much money I'm giving it away. Isn't that right, Nesta?"

My aunt's bright lips pursed. "God's been good to us," she said.

"God, hell," my Uncle Herman said. "He doesn't get up to take the night calls."

My father had found his cigarette and with a clear look of relief sat up straight on the hassock. He laughed. "You're right there, Herman," he said.

"You wouldn't believe it, Fred," my uncle said. "You would not believe it. I got these two kids now, fresh out of interneship, and what do you think, do they want to run around taking the night work? Oh no, not these kids."

"They want a good salary from Herman but they don't want to work for it," my Aunt Nesta said. "Herman's worked hard all these years, and I want him to take it easy now. After all, these younger kids should take over some of the burden."

Herman waved his cigar, excusing, temporarily, his dilatory help. "One good thing about a big-city practice, you keep up with the times. I'll bet you people out here haven't even heard of penicillin yet. It's the big thing. I give it to everybody for everything—colds, headaches, female complaints. Everybody comes in, 'How about a shot of penicillin, Doc?' Sure, sure. It's the new age of miracles. If anybody's sick nowadays, the doctor's to blame. Nobody should have to suffer three-four days with a head cold. Well, if that's what they want, that's what I give. It's good psychology, makes the patient feel good, know what I mean? He thinks he's getting all the latest stuff. The way they used to let blood. Ah, medicine these days is three quarters psychology, one quarter business. Or maybe fifty-fifty. Keep 'em happy, that's my idea." He blew out a large brown cloud of smoke and spat a bit of tobacco from his lip. My father, at a loss, blinked.

"I can't believe," he said, "that you'd really give any drug indiscriminately."

"Good old Fred," my uncle said and laughed.

"Herman's just talking, Fred," my mother said. "You ought to know Herman by this time. He's just fooling."

"Who's fooling," my uncle said indignantly, and winked.

My mother rose in a flustered rustle of silk. "Who would like a nice cold drink? I'm sure the boys must be thirsty."

My father got up and said, "Herman, how about a tour of the premises? I've got some interesting things to show you. I don't know if Frieda's written you, but I've been doing some interesting work on various clinical problems."

"Fred," my mother said, "why don't we all have some ginger ale first?"

"Say," my cousin Henry said, "what time's this show get on the road? It's almost three."

"It couldn't be that late," my mother said. "Oh dear, we've got to get right over to the church. Eleanor, go up and get Sully, please."

My Uncle Herman had gotten up and stomped inside to inspect the dining room. As I went up the stairs to get Sully, I heard him calling to my mother, "Small wedding, eh, Frieda?" I didn't hear my mother's reply.

The church, built of thick gray stone and ivy-covered, is cold even in June and dark even at three this afternoon. I stand next to my sister in the chancel's dimness. The windows, tall watchful candles, dapple her golden arms blue, send licks of cooled flame shifting across her snowy skirts. Under the frosty fall of veil her face is lifted, calm. I tremble. Words hang here, simple, smooth, weighty as stones, questions demanding answers. Which suddenly and simply is done. Then, with conscious creak and groping, clumsy rustle, the bride is sought and kissed. The organ showers us with sudden music. We turn. Now billowing swiftly, white, her skirts, still dappled, sail before me and this long aisle rushing under us seems a maroon river, and we strange voyagers, and they on either side, solemn natives, awestruck, ceremoniously dressed, and then, before us, doors are hastily opened, lids sprung back on bright boxes of sunlight. There our goal, the shimmering open sea of summer air.

. . . . .

But what I remembered sadly was that my mother, when we passed her, had not looked up. She gazed at the floor, thinking of something else. Still, at home she was very gay. Her hair loosened and fell engagingly over one eye. She laughed, showing charming, crooked teeth, and her small explosions of laughter lit the room. Kindled thus, the party grew hilarious. Toasts were made and drunk, the cake cut and eaten. My uncle joked and hugged plump Mrs. Flipman who gasped as she laughed and with fat, red-tipped fingers delicately pressed the gaping neckline of her orange dress. Morosely, Mr. Flipman remembered dull tales from Bill's childhood. Cheerfully, my father told a cornered guest why liquor, cigarettes, and beef would kill him and I, left alone, drank champagne, wanting out of curiosity, to get smashed. I finished my first glass quickly, set it down, took up the next and looked around to make sure no one saw. All clear. But there, next to the rubber plant, Mrs. Flipman's nephew, a thin, blond boy scowling at me. Well, what of it, I thought, and scowled back. He had come alone, without his parents, as a kindness, one felt, of the Flipmans; parentless, he was therefore also powerless. Yet it was hard to tell what a boy this age might say, they were so unformed.

"Here," I said, thrusting the glass at him, "you want it?"

"I had some," he said.

"You can have more than one," I offered, dispensing hospitality.

"No, thanks," he said. I shrugged and nonchalantly sipped.

"What's the matter," he said, "your mother won't let you have any?"

"I can have all I want."

"You better not drink too much, you'll get a headache from it."

"I suppose you drink it every day. For breakfast."

"I had it a couple of times. I like beer better."

I studied him. He was about my age and didn't shave yet. He had on queer clothes—a man's navy-blue suit, heavily padded in the shoulders, a bright tie striped in yellow and black. The cuffs of his shirt stuck out and were fixed with huge ruby studs.

"Are you a Cliftonian?" I asked.

"Huh? Speak English, for crying out loud."

"Do you live here in Clifton, New York, is what I asked."

"Sure, where'd you think? I live up on Cassell Street."

"You don't go to the junior high school, do you?"

"Nah, I go to St. Stan's. It's a lousy school, the nuns are too strict. Do anything wrong you get whacked with a lousy ruler. Next year I'm going to public school, the high school, I mean. It's closer to where I live anyhow. This house all belong to you?"

"Well, who did you think?" I said, my voice falling into the boy's strange rudeness.

"How do I know? What do you need so much room for?"

"My father's office is downstairs, and there's only one bedroom on this floor. The rooms are big. Our bedrooms,

Sully's and mine, are upstairs on the third floor. After tonight I'll have the whole third floor to myself."

"Yeah? Gee, you ought to rent some of the rooms."

"Rent them. What for?"

"You don't need 'em all. You could make money."

"My mother wouldn't dream of having strange people in the house," I said. "She's just that kind, she needs privacy."

He shrugged and after a silent moment said, "I've got a great room. It's full of furniture, this maple furniture, and the whole room's made out to look like a boat, know what I mean? The bed's got this wheel at the head, see, and—uh—the curtains are blue. They got these ropes and wheels all over 'em. I got a picture of a sailboat on the wall, and you know what else?"

"No," I said.

"A ship in a bottle."

"Really," I said, laconically.

"Yeah, my father made it. That's his hobby. You ought to see him, the way he puts those things together. Hey, what time is it? I gotta go." He craned his neck looking for a clock. I looked for the clock that usually sat on the buffet, but today it had been replaced by the wedding cake, now a shaky shambles of crumbs and frosting.

"You're not supposed to leave yet," I told him. "You're supposed to wait until the bride leaves."

"I gotta be home," he said. He reached for the last poured glass of champagne on the table, and drank it without stopping. He put it down and said loudly, "Not as good as beer but better'n nothing. See you around." And without saying good-bye to anyone, me, or his aunt, or my mother, or Sully and Bill, he turned and walked out through the crowd to the door.

"Well, good-bye to you, idiot," I called after him. I turned around. My Aunt Nesta was watching me. I scowled and picked at the stalk of the rubber plant, and pushed myself back into the wall.

"Frieda," I heard my aunt say, "I think you're wonderful to give your girls such freedom, but I think Eleanor has had too much to drink."

A little later Sully and Bill left. Sully wore a yellow daisy corsage on her brown linen suit and they drove off in their loaded Chevy, with the U-Haul-It full of wedding gifts. The Schlegels left immediately. We were, after all, a detour on their route. They were on the way to Lake Placid and had, as Uncle Herman said, just dropped off Route 5.

Still in her mauve silk dress but with her shoes off, my mother was walking back and forth from the dining room to the kitchen, carrying trays of glasses and cake plates and forks. My father was stretched out in one of the hidden easy chairs—it was tucked in the corner between the buffet and the door—and I was in another misplaced chair.

"Daddy," I asked. "Where's Cassell Street?"

"Cassell?" he said, and thought. "Cassell, Cassell. Why? Who lives there?"

"This boy Stephen. Mrs. Flipman's nephew. Is it up off Hill Street?"

"Cassell, let's see. Of course, yes, Wierzbicki, in thirty-seven, or was it eight? Pneumonia, I believe it was, with an abscess on the right lung, lower lobe. No, it's nowhere near Hill Street. It's up on Polish Hill next to the mills. Yessir. Right in the middle of the hog's gut."

"What?" I said.

"Never mind," my mother said. "Just don't bother taking one of your tours up there."

"Frieda," my father complained, "why don't you sit down? The crumbs will all be here tomorrow."

"I can't, I can't," my mother said. "I'm too nervous to sit down. I told Sully to call me in the morning. I know I shouldn't have, but that boy is so full of bubbles he's likely to drive into the river."

"They were just happy," my father said. He sat up, reached into the left side pocket of his dark-blue suit, brought out a small round bottle, pulled out the plastic plug, shook two pink pills into his hand, swallowed them, and sank back into the chair.

"They *were* happy," my mother said, loading her tray again. "I think they were *really* happy."

"Of course they were," my father said. "Anyone with sense could see that. They wanted to get married."

"It wasn't a"—she glanced in my direction and shrugged—"shotgun wedding."

"Of course not," my father said, "everybody understood that."

"I didn't hear any talk," my mother said, "and, well, what if there was?"

"There's always talk," my father said. "People don't have anything else to think about."

My mother went past me, carrying the tray. "Still," her voice came floating to us from the kitchen, "they're so young. I wish they'd waited."

My father raised one hand. "It's over with, Frieda." He laughed suddenly and my mother, coming back into the room with a grave look, said, surprised, "What?"

"I was just thinking. What was the name of that fellow Herman wanted to marry you off to? The one whose father had the big butcher market?"

"Rudy Hilfreich," my mother said promptly. My father raised his head to look at her; this promptness, I guess, had made him uneasy. My mother with a calm, chaste look went by him into the kitchen.

"That's right," he said, looking after her. "What an idea."

"Who was he, Mother?" I called.

"Two hundred and ten pounds of pure beef," my father answered.

"He wasn't at all fat," my mother said, coming back into the room. "He was . . . large. Big-boned."

"Had beef for a brain, too," my father said.

"Oh, he did not," my mother said, irritated. "He just didn't have much education. He was very clever at butchering. I understand he's a rich man today."

"Why not? Millions have been made on the black market."

"Oh, Fred, honestly."

"No, Frieda, dishonestly. He used to eat four meals a day at Schlegel's restaurant, just to see your mother."

"Your father used to eat there, too," my mother said.

"I could only afford to eat every other day," my father said. "Your mother," he said to me, as if I hadn't heard this all before, "used to make change at Schlegel's. There she was behind the cigars, and the mints, and toothpicks, and that big fancy black register, and she'd make your change, you see, and never look up. Always had her head down in a book. I ate there a month before I saw her face. She had her hair—it was blond in those days—all twisted back in these braids." To demonstrate, he craned his neck coyly and looped with his forefingers the circumference of his ears.

"Your father," my mother said, starting to smile, "used to come in straight from the hospital. He'd always have blood spots on his coat. His bill was the same every day: liver, onions, noodles, and two coffees, thirty-five cents."

"What an extravagance that second cup was," my father said, shaking his head.

"The first time we went out your father took me to the opera. They were singing 'Tristan.' It rained and out of vanity I hadn't worn boots, and your father had spent so much on the tickets that he couldn't afford a cab. We waited hours and hours in the pouring rain for the trolley, and I ruined my shoes. Remember that, Fred?"

"All I remember is not eating for days afterward." He put his hand over his stomach, as though hunger pains had begun again. "Then I used to think there was nothing better than liver, now I'm sure it ruined my gut."

"It was France, Fred, you know that."

"No, Frieda, not France, Shigella and the war. Good old Shigella. All these goddamn wars." He took off his glasses, opened his snap case, and took out the piece of pinked cloth he used to wipe his glasses. Carefully, he replaced his glasses, then got up and began helping my mother, who was lifting the edges of the lace cloth, shaking it a little so the crumbs would stay in the center. Then he put his hand to his stomach, his mouth puckered, and he left the room. We heard the bathroom door slam. My mother continued to lift up the cloth and I got up to take my father's place.

"He's upset," she said, in a tone she seldom took, explaining my father to me. She reached for my end of the cloth and bunched it all together.

"And you work too hard, Mother," I said.

She looked surprised and caught the wadded cloth against her breast. "Do I? Oh, I don't think so. Why what would I do if I didn't work? I don't play bridge, I don't play golf. I've got to do something." She looked at me and smiled, a wavery replica of her smile of the afternoon. "I hope you won't have to do my kind of work, though. Not that I don't like it, it's all right for me, but for you there'll be so many more interesting things to do. And I do wonder sometimes what this business is all about, getting married, raising children. What for? You look back and you've spent your life at it. You don't remember whether it was pleasant or rewarding or not. It's just something you've done, the only thing. Oh, this endless reproduction. Does it make sense?" She shook her head and then, as if her thoughts had reverted to a truer plane, said, "Well, she'll find out. Now I hope *you* won't do anything foolish," and she turned and went straight-backed into the kitchen and then onto the porch. I could see her from where I stood, vigorously shaking the lacy cloth into the June night, the crumbs scattering among the darkly shining leaves of the pear tree.

I went upstairs but instead of going to sleep put on my bedside light to read. From the kitchen I heard the rattle of the dishpan and the rush of water in the pipes. Then it was quiet. Occasionally, small bugs plopped against the screen. Occasionally, I stopped at turning a page to listen. For years, reading illegally, too late, I had listened for my sister's heave upon the springs. Her breath, rising from her window to descend into mine had, with its heavy, even, sealike soughing, provoked my word-botched hours. Now her breath mingled with her husband's and I was left alone, to cope with and absorb the problems of this household. Now there were no small noises, only the heavy stillness of a warm June night. I could not sleep and so I read and the light of the bedside lamp seemed to make a white hourglass through which, little by little, the darkest hours of the night were sifted.

PART II

I

Fall tonight, suddenly cold and foggy. Downtown here the smell of river damp is everywhere. There is no wind. Windows are down, doors are closed, house is quiet. No sound of cars, people, Elks Club dance band, Mohawkin Mills machines. Sounds are closed out, we are closed in. Silence. This house is cold. Heat Costs Money.

On coldest third floor I read in bed on last free night before school. Nose runny, fingers cold. Under wad of blankets legs cramp and book slides down the quilted hump my knees make. This cold funny quiet room. Funny the inside slope of wall, the small high windows. Wallpaper once pink and silver, stripes alternating with daisy chains, now aging fragilely in tones of beige and brown. My little-girl desk, white, scratched; my bureau, with a bunny decal on it; my peeling white-painted iron bed; and in my closet, collections of stones, stamps, magazines, letters to foreign pen pals, junk. My room, though. My junk. My quiet.

Downstairs father sits and reads. Makes small noises: Oh! Aha! Scratches, stares at ceiling, turns a page. Mother sits and sews in orange light of table lamp. Shears squeak, she snaps thread. Waiting. Worries. Silence. Worries a heavy presence. No one rings waiting-room bell. Silence. Worries. Money. practice falling off. Silence. Sully, three years married, doesn't write. Silence. Louis now five years dead. Silence.

This house built 1892 by Grandfather Munson. Solid construction, solid walls three bricks deep, three floors, fourteen rooms, ceilings are fourteen feet high. Floors are double, don't creak. Funny. He left no money, just this house. Died 1918 of influenza. Left cracked widow to be cared for. She religious nut. Everything a sin. Smoking, drinking, movies, love. Stood up in church on Palm Sunday to catechize minister. Walked the streets of Clifton muttering, carried a shopping bag full of pamphlets, tracts, admonitions, prophecies. Dressed only in black. Died in fall down back stairs, 1926. Father married, finally, '27. After four-year engagement. Then Louis born. Oh, all different maybe if Louis were alive. Big old Louis. Big, German-looking, but no Stoic. A tease, laughed a lot. Always knew jokes, some dirty. A whistler, sang, picked out tunes on piano. Big gentle boy. Wrestler and football. Did math, liked science. Never read fiction or poetry. Took long showers in morning, left bathroom steamy, towels spongy, soap like glue, unpleasant tepid pools on floor. I smelled him again at dinner. Like men who smell like human beings. Like men. Hate girls in crowds. Afraid of them. Hates girls' basketball (left guard), don't like girls to touch me, or to touch them. When boys touch, I jump. Was it on the first day of school last year that we collided, Stephen and I? Our eyes flew together, nested briefly, then flew apart. Funny I didn't recognize him, he was so suddenly tall. Love each other? He is silent. No gabber. Hate men gabbers. S. quiet. Funny face, long broken nose, curly lips, cold eyes. Want to look at him all the time. Beautiful the way he plays his game, makes perfect moves on court and then after free shot, walking so loose, head bent, hand on hip, and then running again, dribbling ball, so easy. His mother, they say, is a whore. Love him perhaps but don't want to marry. Don't ever want to marry. Love a lot and have fat sweet children but no marriage. Makes women bitter, men strange. Want to travel, have money, buy clothes that fit, a cashmere sweater, have own library, favorite books bound in soft brown leather. Be independent. Travel: Bangkok, Kashmir, Madrid, Rome, see also Germany, my mother's country. Hard people, the Germans. Stoics. Duty. Obedience. Respect for laws. Cowards, also. Hard working, though. Oh, lovely to see him work math problems, down, down, down the board, right hand stuck in back pocket, left held squawking chalk, everyone watching, smaller and smaller and smaller, stripping to a small bare nut, so easy he peeled. Often looked at me, said nothing. Why? His mother, they say, is a whore. Mine not. Nothing there. I guess you don't need it after thirty-five. Poor mother, poor woman. Lift must be empty, sterile, flat. God save me from same. Want to know, see, do, feel, everything. So cold in house tonight, so still.

2

"Hi, Charles," I say. "Beautiful day, what?"

"Aha!" Charlie says. "So you're back." He is standing in the doorway of his place smoking a cigar and looking like a meat packer, black-haired and burly under his long white apron. "Weren't you just here a coupla months ago? Whatsa matter, you got no home?"

"It's you, Charlie," I say, "you're so magnetic. Did you miss me?"

"Yeah yeah," he says gloomily and tips the ash off his cigar. "I had a hunnert kids here, no kidding, every night, all summer long. Every old lady on the street complain about the noise."

"I'll bet you loved it," I say and sit down on the long concrete step of the porch, arranging my books next to me in a neat pile. "Patty Byers been by yet?"

"Byers? Nah. Go home, go home, is all I yell, all summer. Whatsa matter, you kids got no home? Think you was all orphans. Least when the high school starts up you got someplace to go in the daytime. Or if you'd anyways buy something."

"I did buy something," I say. "I believe it was last June. Probably a Coke."

"Big spenders," he says. "I'm gonna die a millionaire," and he turns into the store. He goes behind the counter and starts polishing Coke glasses with a dish towel. As if anyone will use them. When the kids come, they buy their Cokes from the cooler so they can take them out to the steps where everyone sits. On a good night there'll be fifteen, twenty kids outside. The inside's too small, only three stools and one booth crammed between the cooler and the pocket-book spin rack. As soon as it gets cold, the kids'll start going down to City Drug where there are eight or nine booths, and a real fountain, and a juke box. This is Charlie's big time, spring, summer, early fall. He's funny, though. As soon as the races start at Saratoga he closes up, rents a room there and stays as long as his money lasts. That's his real passion, horses. He's got a girlfriend, too, a kind of nice-looking fat blonde, I see them together sometimes on Sundays. But every summer he leaves everything, even her, for the nags. Most of the time he sits in the back of the store with his chair tilted up against the wall reading the *Morning Telegraph*.

I pick up my algebra book from the top of the stack and flip it open. There they are again, all those awful x's I thought I'd left behind in junior high school. I take a bent Pall Mall from the pack I bought last Friday and smoke and pretend to be studying the book because not to would look peculiar, as if I were just hanging around. Charlie's is on a small side street of neat white houses and every few minutes I look up to watch the little kids across the road. They are playing a careful game of gardening, dragging a sandpail full of water from the spigot at the side of the house to the front lawn where they have dug some holes. A long blue car, shark-nosed, glides between me and the kids and Patty's father leans out of the car window and waves. Ugh. Snail-like, I feel myself contact. Pig. I hate him and his glinty smile. One night last May—the night of my fifteenth birthday—we were sitting on Patty's porch in the dark pretty late, drinking root beer, and the Byers having high-balls, and to celebrate, Patty's mother said we could each have half a weak one, and while we were drinking them, sitting there in the dark, he put his hand on my leg. I had shorts on and he kept sliding his hand up until it was near the edge of my shorts. I sat there, with my knees locked together, not knowing what to do, and feeling his sweaty palm on the top of my thigh. And I didn't do anything. Because he was Patty's father. God, I hate men that age. Oh well, poor old Byers. It must be awful to be that age and maybe I won't live that long. It's the worst age to be, a kind of no man's land between where you'd hoped to be going and where you know you are. The two little kids are watering each other now with a hose, illegally, I'll bet, because they have on blue jeans and polo shirts. Yes, here comes their mother, banging out of the door and down the steps. She's young, Sully's age, and reminds me of Sully, with her bare feet and Bermuda shorts too tight in the rear. She yanks each child by an elbow and hauls them off squealing up the steps. The screen door slams. I hear the noise of their protest wind up the stairs and then a car stops at the corner of my vision and I panic thinking it's Byers again. But no. It's a car I don't know, a black Plymouth, whale-shaped like all the post-war Plymouths, and then I see who it is, and I look down at the algebra very studiously, and turn the unread page and then, very nonchalant, look up. Ronnie Wilkins jumps out on the curb side and then from around the other side he comes. Stephen. They're laughing about something and I put my head down again. As they come up the steps, I see only their long sneakered feet. Ronnie has tennis shoes on but *he* has on those old black high-top things, held together with gray knotted string. They both wear cuffless khakis.

"Well, what do you know," Ronnie says, his sneakers climbing past me. "Meatball's here. Hey, look at that, will you? The poor girl's been dragging her books around with her, she can't bear to part with them, not even on the first day of school." They go inside. "Charlie, old buddy," Ronnie says, "put two on the nose for Red Fern," and Charlie doesn't think that's funny, he's been investigated twice though he's clean.

"Get what you want, sonny, and leave me alone," Charlie says to him. I hear the bottles in the cooler clink and then the plip of the caps dropping into the holder. They come out. I turn very slightly, just enough to see Stephen slide his whole long length down against the side of the store, then close his eyes, and put his face up to the sun. I have to look away he has such an honest-to-God beautiful face. Behind him, Ronnie, a freckled satyr, leans grinning in the doorway. With a thumb over the mouth of the Coke bottle he is shaking it to make it foam and holds it threateningly toward me.

"Catch," he says. "What'd you do all summer, Meatball? You're not as obese as you used to be."

"I taught small children how to swim," I say coolly and turn another page of the algebra and study it closely.

"No fooling, "Ronnie says, "so it wasn't fat after all, it was muscle. Wojcik, we'll have to start calling Meatball 'Muscles.' Hey, did I tell you I saw her old man last week?" Stephen, eyes still closed, shakes his head. He raises his Coke and takes a long swallow. "I'm in City Drug see, with Marilyn Polito. You know her, Steve, huh?" His hands lasciviously scoop Polito's shape from the hot September air. "Well, we're sitting in that back booth, see, the one nearest prescriptions, and having a little fun, nothing serious, when in comes Meatball's old man. He blinks at us and runs down to the counter and Marilyn looks at him and laughs. What's wrong, I ask, but she gives me an elbow in the side. Pretty soon he gets his bundle of pills and turns around and Marilyn's sitting there choking, with her hand over her teeth. The zipper's stuck, see, about halfway up. Geez, I woulda run after him to tell him, but I didn't have the heart. I mean, the poor guy. He'd probably been walking around like that all day."

My eyes by now have begun to blur from staring so hard at the page. Behind me, Charlie's broken radio crackles and the flat voice of the man who announces local news brays on about the Wooldyers' next home game. I pick up my stack of books. To get down the step I have to walk over Stephen's outstretched feet, and I look straight at him and give him, I don't know why, all the hate I meant for Ronnie. He looks up at me. Nothing on his face changes, as if he were and weren't looking at me.

"Excuse *me,*" I say. He moves those barge boats one at a time and stares and I go down the step. I walk down the street and I know he's watching me. Strange how his eyes went right up to mine, as if he'd been looking at me all the time. They're very light blue eyes and his hair is a strange white blond. In his face there is a certain remoteness, a cold secrecy I love. I keep my back straight and I'm glad I wore this dress, the color of young moss, and I'm glad I'm very tanned. This is my best time of year, my hair has streaked to blond and I feel burnished, dipped in a dark sunshine, a golden girl, and nothing can touch me, nothing, unless I want it to.

3

Halfway down the block I hear Patty Byers call. I turn to watch her come up, her black watch kilt tumbling too far above her knees and her face pale except for the inflamed flanges of her nose.

"Well, hi, old girl," I say. "How goes the ragweed?"

She shrugs and shifts her books, searching the cuff of her rolled-up sleeve for Kleenex. Her eyes run crystal rivers. She snuffles. "Awful. The pollen count must be a billion. And how was your summer?"

"The same. You know. But better than being home."

"Sure. Say, if I'm still alive Saturday I'll have a party. What do you think?"

"Swell."

"You can ask your friend."

"What friend?"

"But if you're smart you won't. I saw him a few times this summer and heard about him a lot. He was very, very busy, your friend."

We begin to walk down the street toward McVey Road. Here, at this corner, we are exactly halfway between the summit of High School Hill and the river. I love to look down from here at this part of town, white, prim houses, set squarely one by one as if in a toy village, and the trees, from this height, the lollipop trees of a child's drawing. All so neat, this town, descending on its grid of streets in the tidy, vertical perspective of an old map, down to meet the river which, S-curved, silver, winds through it like a half-sprung coil.

"He took Marcelline out in July," Patty says, "and I heard he was nothing but hands."

"Give 'em an inch," I say.

"She gives more than that," Patty says and then sighs because, I guess, she hasn't given anything yet. She has pretty pink skin, and black curly hair that springs up live and thick. But she's so terribly tall. She tends to stoop, as if her own height were a burden, and this plantlike tendency is emphasized by the way she carries her books, clutched to her bosom.

The four o'clock whistle blows. At the corner of McVey and Montrose we look toward Houghton's Mills. There, on that side of town, things are different. The houses are cramped in dingy brick rows, with wooden stoops in back, and the back yards just dirt, no grass, and tangles of clotheslines stretching from yard to yard. There are no trees. I've been over there alone maybe once. Kids kids kids everywhere and everything scribbled with chalk. Kids tumbling over porch rails and sitting on the curbstones. Weeds in the cracks of the sidewalks and broken glass in the gutters. Every block has two beer parlors, and that's Cassell Street, where he lives, right across from Houghton's. According to my parents that part of town is sin itself. At night when I lie safe in bed drunkenness, vice, corruption, rage its streets. Now, as if to confirm my elders, the mill's five enormous brick smokestacks give off five simultaneous blasts of smoke. A devil's hand thrusting up from the lower rubble! These funnels of poisonous gray move upward, mushroom and mix into one giant cloud, obscuring God's own blue. I feel more than see this cloud diffuse and let fall on my face a mantle of grit. In my head I hear my father intone, "From Houghton's who shelters us all we must expect such careless benedictions."

"When he took Irene out," Patty says, "they went to the Lake View Drive-Inn, and she's petrified, having heard all from Marcelline, but he doesn't touch her. She scrunches way over in the corner of the seat and they sit all through *The Speckled Thing From Space,* which by the way she's already seen, and at the end of it he drives her home and doesn't say a word. Just reaches over and opens the door and lets her out."

"He smelled fear," I announce briskly to Patty. Somehow, in our relationship I have become the positive one. "Know what this girl at camp, this Julia told me? It's all in the eyes."

Patty looks skeptical. "How in the eyes?"

"She says, if you've got hot eyes they follow you like dogs."

Patty's dark straight brows shoot up. "Swell, but who has hot eyes?"

"You, me, everybody. It's not a gift from God, stupid,

it's like this." I stop and give her the Burning Glance I have been practicing all summer, and she laughs. "Come on," I say. She looks around nervously. The leaves of a maple tree rustle and shift above her, spatter her with an anxious pattern of green and she gives me a burning glance, but it's not very good, more flicker than flame and I say moodily, "It takes practice," and we go on.

But practice is all we do. These past two years, nothing but practice. We must jinx each other, I think. At school they've always called us Meatball (me) and Spaghetti (she). Like me, Patty is smart. We don't like being in the same class because scholarship comes between us, although we manage a good division of interest: she is a math whiz and I do the other things. Our interests overlap in biology—last year Binky had to give us both A. "Now, boyth and girlth, let uth obtherve": these goiterous hags, flat-nosed giants, vitamin-deficient, lizard-skinned freaks. After the midyear, sex. From behind the fuzzy cone of light projected by his sputtering, cranky machine, Mr. Binks's voice issued as if it were the light itself. "You thee—people—uh—how the male the-the-thperm thtruggleth" and the frantic blob on the screen wriggled and there was a deep silent unrest in the class, squeak, squeak, went the lab chairs and no one coughed and when the lights went on again Patty and I kept our faces very still and would not look at Ronnie Wilkins, Stephen Wojcik, or any of the boys. Mr. Binks mopped his brow and hurried to zip up the shade. The bell rang releasing us. There was a sudden hysterical gabble. Patty and I left, very composed, and in the doorway

Wojcik's sweatered elbow grazed my arm and I jumped a mile. I wonder if he's been dating Nora Novak.

We cross Melbourne and are, finally, on Auburn. This is Patty's street, nice, on the good side of the hill. The houses are old, large, comfortable, white, with tall trees and wide lawns. Beds of marigolds line the driveways.

"My father's home," Patty says, and I see Mr. Byers's blue Buick. It is new but scratched and even in front of their house nicks the curb at a sloppy angle. "Want to come in?" she asks. I look up at the porch. Mrs. Byers is there, knitting and wearing a sweater, no matter what she's always cold, and he's there too, slouched down in a chair. There is a drink of something dangling from his hand.

"No," I say, "listen, I've got to get home. There's something I've got to pick up for my mother."

Patty scuffs at a gum wrapper, then conscientiously stoops to pick it up. She wads the scrap in her fist and looks at me, her mouth pursed wisely. "By the way," she says, "I guess I ought to tell you that he took out Nora Novak." She tilts her head, waiting. I shrug. "And you know what that means," she says. I nod, we say good-bye. She walks up the path to the porch and Mrs. Byers lifts her head. I wave and turn and cross the street and walk down the hill toward home.

Even before I get there, I see something's going on. A dusty pick-up truck is parked at the curb and a workman leans against its fender smoking. Both of the front doors are open.

I run up the stone steps and then up the inside stairs. On the second-floor landing my mother is talking to another workman. She seems excited, her hands describe long, then shorter boxes, and she walls them off with short brisk gestures.

"Do you see what I mean, Mr. Schaeffer," she says. She is still in a housedress and over this has put on one of my discarded sweaters, a green elbows-out cardigan. She has on her moccasins and a shoelace is tied around her hair.

"Yeah, I got ya, Miz Munson," Schaeffer says, indulgently. "Long as it conforms. Gonna be trouble on that second bath, though. Gonna have ta break through that middle-room wall."

"Anything," my mother declares, "if it's within my budget. That's all the money I have, Mr Schaeffer, it can't cost a penny more."

I inch past my mother through the door, toss my books into a chair, and go out to the kitchen to get an apple. Starving, always starving. Skipping lunches, I feel like a thin bundle of burning tissue. Hunger seems to speed me up metabolically.

"What's going on," I inquire from behind my mother's back. Good God, why does she wear such awful things? I remember stuffing that sweater in my wastebasket last June. She affects my worn-out clothes as an admonition, I guess, from the generation that still darned socks. "Are we having the house done over? It certainly needs it."

My mother nods at something the man has said and turns an irritated half-face to me.

76

"Is that all, Miz Munson," Schaeffer says, "because the men quit at four and it's nearly five."

"It is? They do? Oh my, it must be wonderful to be a laboring man these days. Well, all right, Mr. Schaeffer, I'll see you tomorrow then, at eight sharp."

"Mother," I say again, "are we having the whole house done? My room too?"

"What?" She turns from Mr. Schaeffer's narrow, paint-spattered coveralls, moving with stiff jauntiness down the stairs, to me. Her energy seems to have waned with his descent and she looks at me wearily.

"Are—we—having the whole house done," I repeat.

She moves past me into the living room. As I look at her she unties the shoelace, and as if it were a working-man's badge and hours were over, drops it into a pocket of the housedress. "Just the third floor," she says and lowers herself slowly onto the piano bench. She sits there tightly, her weight resting forward on her palms. "We're going to break up the third floor into apartments."

"Apartments?"

"To rent. To rent to people to make money." She gets up again and with a small groan straightens her back.

"But what about my room?" I ask.

Her gray eyes, which were blurred with tiredness, now condense calmly. "Saturday I want you to start clearing out your things. I'll put a carton up in the hall. Just take all your junk and dump it in. Clean out that closet. Save a minimum. The men will start up there on Monday."

"Up there?" I say. "In my room? But where am I going to sleep?"

She moves past me toward the kitchen. "You'll have to share my room," she says. "We'll get you a new bed. They have some nice twin bed sets in Dunningers. Why don't we look downtown Thursday—"

"But what will I do with my stuff? The stuff I want to keep? And my clothes?" I wail, following her, disliking myself because I know, I do realize what this is for. Drooping, I watch my mother's back, stiffened against tiredness and me, move toward the kitchen. Without turning toward me, she says, "Don't whine."

4

"Madam," my mother says ironically, standing before me as packed and obdurate as a column, "Miss Byers is on the telephone. Will you take it in the living room?" Hastily, she surveys the closet I have been cleaning. "You mean that's all you've done?"

I mumble something and follow her down the stairs. On the second floor the vacuum and its horde of attachments stand ready for the next offensive—she has almost completed her Saturday assault on dirt. Small tables and chairs have been moved and stand in the middle of the living room, dazed and homeless as villagers caught between armies. As I pick up the phone the whine of the vacuum climbs upward into the earpiece. "Doing" is all I hear.

"What?" I shout.

"What-are-you-doing?" Patty demands.

"Cleaning my closet," I say crossly.

"Come over, why don't you, and help me clean. The rec room's a mess. It'll never be straightened before tonight. Can you come?"

"I told you, Patty, I've got to clean my own room today, because of the carpenters coming."

"Can't you do it later? Tomorrow?"

"On Sunday?"

"All *right,*" she says and there is a tight stretched pause while she waits for me to tell her, but I let her wait and she says, "Well? Is he?"

"What?"

"Oh, stop it. Honestly."

"Yes, I guess he is. He works tonight, though, so he can't pick me up. He said he'd come later."

"No. You're fooling. Aren't you just thrilled?"

"Uh-huh. Listen, Patty, I've got to go."

"Tell me what he said."

"I will, only I've got to go now. My mother'll have a fit"—my mother raises her head from her noisy perusal of the rug—"if the room isn't done."

"Remind me never to give another party, the way I get help from my friends."

"I'm sorry. Truly. Is there anything I can bring?"

"No. Oh, yes. Bring chips. This thing is costing a fortune."

The vacuum whines to a halt. I hang up the phone and go upstairs, my mother's look following me. I haven't told her because she doesn't think girls should ask boys. And I didn't only ask him, I waited an hour for basketball practice to end, swimming laps of the school pool, then, my eyes raw-rimmed from chlorine, my hair oozing droplets down my spine, ran out after him to the steps. There, I called him in front of his friends. He turned. The others ran yowling down the steps to the street, their crimson jackets scattering like petals, and we descended silently together. His face was stern and pale. Stowed under his arm he carried only one book, math, for the entire weekend. I hunched over my six to hide them. I asked him and he said, well, yeah, but he works, he'd have to be late, and I said, well, all right. Then there was nothing to say and then, oddly, at four on this Friday afternoon, church bells rang. We lifted our heads. Below us, chiffon ropes of smoke drifted from Clifton's chimneys. The town lay peaceful, a nineteenth-century, water-color "view"; and now, to bless it and us, this perfect resonance of bells rising from the valley. At the last step he hunched his shoulders, kicked a stone, well, so long, he said, and loped off toward his friends. They turned to look at me and grin. He did not turn, the back of his neck was red. I walked to the Hill Street bus stop. In the back of the jouncing, nearly empty bus, I sat primly with this secret like a sock pulled over my heart, and I didn't want to tell anyone, not even Patty, and least of all my mother.

At ten, my father comes upstairs, still in his bathrobe and slippers.

"Nonsense," he says, "time-consuming nonsense," and he marches toward the storage room. He, too, has been provided with a carton and shuffles back and forth between the room and the hall with inefficient little bundles of things in his hands—a book, a dish of agar-agar, a few dusty test tubes, then comes a pile of notebook papers, scrambled all which-ways, which he tosses into the carton as is, without even a clip. Bottles of medicine, labeled jars, more papers, more books. He dismantles the experiment he has lately set up (he pipes Clifton air through distilled water) and tosses this—clink, clunk—in. He hates change. Judging from the tremor in last night's pipes, his bowels had a bad time. Still, he seems in one of his better humors, grudgingly cheerful. I snap on the radio. This Week's Hundred Top Pops is just going off and Polish Polka Hour coming on, when my mother appears on the stairs. She looks first at my father's carton, but he has deftly and definitely crossed through her thick crayoned OUT and with the thin line of his mechanical pencil written IN.

"You're not going to keep all that," my mother says to my father. She looks at the carton as if it contained a bad smell.

"Certainly," my father says. "I will simply relocate downstairs. Brick by brick by brick. I hope this isn't a maneuver to obstruct my research work."

"Nothing as simple as a move would do it," my mother says and looks into the storage room. This is one room she never goes into, and as she stands at the door I can't tell whether she will laugh or cry. "Dear God," she says and puts her hand to her face. Gradually, as my father's equipment took up more room, as the periphery of his knowledge expanded, the other contents of the room became denser. Broken kitchen chairs were placed on top of each other, boxes were stacked on these. The wobble-legged table held boxes too, and on these were piled old magazines too valuable to be thrown away. Here and there, boots, old games, toys. From a box three up peeps the blue corner of Parker Brothers' *Sorry,* a galosh, unbuckled, sticks out of a carton, and from a box marked Clothes—old the recrudescence of a certain red bathrobe makes me remember the winter I was nine and nearly died of bronchitis. All of this stuff has been heaped at the back of the room, piled precariously into a towering wall against the windows. It looks like one of those crazy booby-trap barriers that eccentrics erect against the world.

"I suppose what we should do," my mother says, "is to call Mr. Iffoletti and have him haul it all away." But she edges past my father and squats at the bottom of the cliff and tugs open a corner of a box. She looks, pushes the flap back, straightens. "Yes," she says firmly, "that's what we'll do. It would take weeks to sort through this."

"Sell it," my father says. He is standing in the storage-room doorway with a beaker and a raw potato. "Sell it and we'll make a fortune, as I suppose we're going to do as soon as our rich tenants move in."

"Never mind the rich," my mother says, coming back out into the hall. "All they have to do is pay the rent."

My father snorts. "And who do you suppose is going to move in? Blake Ritchie? Edmund Houghton?"

"I don't care who, I don't care," my mother says, "as long as they're clean and quiet and pay."

"Well, I care," my father says. "I have a vision of a large drunken millworker sitting on our third-floor porch, throwing his beer bottles down into my garden."

"Oh, Fred," my mother says, "why would you care? You haven't been in the garden for years."

"Or," my father goes on, "some warped old maid who arises at five every morning to go to church. My God, Frieda, anything but a religious fanatic."

"Now what do you mean by that? Catholic? Do consider, Fred, that the population of this town is eighty-three per cent Catholic. Though I can't see why you're worried. You sleep like a drowned man from four A.M. until ten. And *they're* going to be up here, *you're* going to be down there." She begins to tug at the carton to which my father is still making his inept sacrifices. I help her and together we shove the box to the stairs.

"Be careful," she says to me, and I'm not sure whether it's me she's worried about or the box; she thinks of me as both very frail and incapable, and as we begin to tilt the box to get it down the stairs my father shuffles over to help. Inanimate things retract in his presence and at his touch the box seems to jump toward my mother. My mother, standing backward on the stairs, teeters, the box tips, I dig in and hold on, my mother clutches the bannister.

"Fred," she cries, "for heaven's sake, let go!" Alarmed, my father leaps back, the box seemingly rights itself, and my mother and I begin working it carefully down the stairs while my father peers anxiously at us over the railing.

By seven that night the closet shelves are bare, my meager possessions stashed in a cleared drawer of my mother's bureau. Lying in the third-floor bathtub under a blanket of cold bubbles I feel stripped of my childhood. Next to go, this bathroom, thanks be. It will be nice to have hot water.

Water on the way to the third floor gains color and loses heat, so that this tub, porcine in character, with a curvaceous middle and dainty claw feet, has, as well, a rust streak down its gullet. The toilet is another antique, flushed by pulling on a long chain. Thereupon, the tank hiccoughs and burbles like a babe and you wait to repeat the process. It takes two pulls to achieve ablution and I remember that it once took Louis half an hour to flush a dead garter snake. For a long time after that I avoided using the third-floor john. Fear of resurrection, I guess. It's a big room, though, all aristocratic space and feudal inconvenience. When we were small we had water fights in here. When Sully still lived here we fought over the division of the shelf under the mirror, her bottles, creams, ointments, lotions, and pastes always encroaching on my shampoo. When Sully lived here she had the early Saturday bath so she could get out, and it seems queer to me that seven is now my hour. This crazy bathroom, ugly with apple-green walls, and the tiles around the tub chipped à la the Clifton RR station WC, and, like a Rand McNally relief map, the orange-and-green linoleum, all blackened craters and unexplainable heaves. But I have peeled many a layer of childhood here and years of familiarity abrade ugliness and I am thinking this when my mother knocks at the door and comes in. She is carrying a large stack of towels and looks at me over them. The look is pinched.

"Didn't you just take a bath this morning?" I read on her face, Hot Water Costs Money.

"This morning? No, I merely washed my hair." The

water is now totally tepid and although I'd rather not reveal myself, I lunge out of the suds and make a long reach for the bath towel which I have slung over the shower-curtain rod. As I pull it down, the rod wobbles, and a little plaster dust sifts slowly to the floor. My mother looks at it and then at me. For the second time that day she puts her hand to her face.

"Dear God, Eleanor, how much do you weigh?" Her look of shock delights me.

"One-twenty?" I say. "I don't know, I'm a horse." I weigh one-fifteen but don't want to cause a panic.

"You're nothing but bones," she says, and reaching out, feels my clavicle.

"Really, Mother," I say and hike the towel up higher.

"You're not eating," she accuses, and begins draping towels over the bars in the bathroom. "You don't eat your dinner and you probably don't eat lunch. I suppose it was lunch money that bought that new sweater?"

"Christmas money," I say weakly, and mutter, "I save my allowance." I jerk the chain plug of the tub with my toe. "You know what we need, Mother dear, is a new hot water heater. The H_2O up here is practically frigid."

"You let me worry about the maintenance," she says. "I've been janitress long enough to know my job. Eleanor, we all do foolish things when we're young, things we regret later on." I turn my back to dry my front and she says, "Remember, there's nothing more important than good health. If you insist on looking like a *Vogue* scarecrow, you may end up flat on your back at Saranac. Don't smirk, there's lots of t.b. still around and let me tell you, it's a living death." She sighs, her speech over. My mother is a bug on t.b. because when she was nineteen she got it and had to spend six months in a sanitorium. That's how she first got to know my father well. When he found out why she wasn't working in Schlegel's he went up to see her, took the train from New York City to Utica and from there up into the Adirondacks. It was a long trip then, took about twelve hours. I have a picture of my mother sitting at the bottom of a totemlike tobogganful of people. She is wearing a white turtleneck sweater and knickers and argyle knee socks. Now she sits on the radiator studying me warily, her hands on her knees. I hop out of the tub still in my terry sarong, and start pulling bobby pins out of my hair.

"Is it Patty who's having the party?" she asks.

"Mmm," I say.

"What time will it be over?"

"I don't know, exactly. After eleven. Maybe around twelve."

"Then I suppose your father should pick you up?"

"Heavens, Mother, don't be silly. He never has before." With my palm I sweep a space in the steamy mirror and her face comes through over my shoulder, pained and anxious like the woman in the aspirin ads.

"Someone's got to see you home. Will Patty's father take you?"

Involuntarily, I shiver.

"What's wrong?" my mother asks sharply.

"Cold," I say. "The thing is, some boy will probably

take me home. As a matter of fact, a boy I know said he would."

"Oh," my mother says. She folds her arms across her bosom and leaned forward thoughtfully. Her lips purse. "Is he coming to get you too?"

"Well, no," I say. "He works in a store on Saturday nights so he'll be late."

"I see," she says, as if that explained everything, but she holds her keening position and her face is still somewhat cramped. Then she shakes her head and gets up. In passing the bathtub she looks at it vaguely, then draws back startled. To my shame, she bends and vigorously starts to scrub the tub with a rag.

"Oh dear," I say, "I'll do that. Really I will."

"No matter," she says. "What's his name? Do we know him?"

"No, you don't really know him. He's a cousin of Bill's—Bill Flipman's—but you haven't met him, not really. He came to Sully's wedding, but he's changed a lot since then. Then he was short."

"Now he's tall."

"Yes, kind of. I mean, he is. He plays basketball."

"I suppose that means he's giant-size. What's his name?"

"Wojcik," I say.

She nods, goes on scrubbing at the tub as if it's a protesting boy, then wrings out the rag, shakes it, and hangs it over the tub's side to dry. She walks to the door. I sigh, but too soon. Her hand on the door is tentative.

"Is he Catholic?"

I groan out loud.

"No," she says, "now you listen. I know you won't believe me, but I feel I have to say this anyway. If he's a good Catholic he's too religious for you, and if he's not, he'll try anything. These halfway Catholics! They think they're going to confess it all later and save their souls."

"What about the halfway Protestants?" I ask her. "Don't you worry about them?"

"Of course I do, I worry about them all. No man's perfect and there are lots of them who won't remember your name in the morning."

Wise as I am, it takes me a minute to drink this in. Then I feel a terrific blush rise upward from the edge of the towel. I stare at her. It's as if, all at once, she's robbed me of the teens I want to believe in, the pastel world of proms and throb-throated boys. I hate her saying this. I don't want to think about sex. I want to have a good time.

She turns her head away. "I'm sorry," she says. "I'm upset tonight. All I want you to do is act sensibly. Think of your future." She attempts a smile. "After all, in a way, your future is all I have." Then, firmly, calmly, like a minister shutting the Bible at the end of scriptures, she straightens, opens the door, and closes it quietly behind her.

5

The Byerses' rec room is really a cellar, just whitewashed plasterboard covering the walls, and a concrete floor painted battleship gray. There are a few folding chairs, and the garden things, rusted wrought-iron benches brought in to winter here. They are full of hidden thorns. Most of us sit on the stairs. Patty has covered her ping-pong table with a red-check cloth, and the cloth is covered with plates of food: Swiss cheese, ham, salami, a jar of mustard, a bowl of pickles, a basket of bread. There are Cokes, but everyone drinks beer. I tend the prewar phonograph, cautiously handling a brittle Bing seventy-eight. "You keep coming back like a song," he groans, everyone moans, Fred Simmons moos like a cow.

Now, at nine, all shoes are off, but only Patty and Peter Harris are dancing. He loves her, she hates him. He is pink and fat, a perspiring cherub, and so short for her that she holds her head awkwardly, in the position of a doting mother. They part, Patty flees. Flushed Peter gropes for food, builds a huge sandwich and burrows into it, hiding. The boys who brought the beer pad up and down the stairs, caring for it. They get cold cans out of the refrigerator and put warm ones in the freezer for quick chilling. Grace Martin comes toward me, her breasts in the white sweater advancing as steadily as two hoplites. Why do you suppose those guys bother to come, she asks me, jerking her head in the direction of the stairs. All they do is play poker. Mrs. Byers finds out she'll have a fit—you know what a Baptist she is. Grace's bright chocolate eyes are restless; her fleshy upper lip with its dark down fringe curves petulantly. She is known as a loose necker and will, on an evening such as this, succor any boy for a few hours. We forgive her this. She claims later, her dark eyes shriveling, that, honest, she just can't drink beer and besides, she is in other ways equally generous. A great lender of money, apparel, nail polish, and homework, which she does with indifference but correctly. She's a natural brain but doesn't enjoy thinking. Now she snaps her fingers in time to the music and moodily bobs her head. It's ten fifteen and Stephen still has not come. I get Grace to watch the phonograph and grab my coat from the closet under the stairs and go up to the kitchen. The kitchen is full of yellow smoke, the oilcloth-covered table littered with heaped ashtrays, punctured beer cans, piles of poker chips and change, and crossed, socked feet. Ronnie Wilkins is smoking a big cigar and tilts back his chair as I pass.

"Hey, Muscles," he leers, "stick around. We're just about to start a game of strip." I pass by him into the short hall, and then into the living room. It is dark, hot-house damp, alive with the warmth of mixed breathing. On all the chairs, on the loveseat, on the sofa, are bulky huddled shapes. I look straight ahead and reach for the cold brass doorknob. Puritan. And I thought I had become immune to other people's careless lovings. This is what comes of living so much at home.

I walk down the path quickly, my heels sounding strict as a teacher's. The street is dark. From a house across the way blinks the diamond-blue eye of a TV. I have seen the couple who live there, young with young children. Not even thirty, is my guess. You'd think they'd have more to do on a Saturday night, but that's the way Clifton is. Awful to be that age and have everything already decided, life over except for the living. But that's the way Clifton is. Every day here in Clifton is the same. Day after day, year after year. Grow up, get married, die here. Daily life. Work and eat. Everywhere I guess the world turns on simple things. Economics. Millions of souls the world over working to eat, excrete, eat again. Endless centuries, chains of mortal generations, all to what end? Where is the world of passion, elegance? Passion at twenty, but at thirty, elegance. Correspondence on thick creamy paper, polished mahogany tables, yellow roses in a silver bowl.

"Hey!"

I turn, squint, pretend to see nothing, walk on. There is running behind me.

"For Christ's sake," he yells and comes up to my side.

"Oh, hello," I say. "Were you looking for me?"

"Looking! I've been all over the damn hill. What a nutty thing to do."

I shrug, look down, observe the suede toe of my shoe. "I didn't think you were coming."

"No?"

"No."

"I said I would, didn't I?"

"You said you'd *try*. Anyway, I didn't go far."

"I went the other way first, *down* Hill Street. I thought you'd gone home." His shoe, square as a box with a thick ridge of sole, angrily punches a leaf. "We going to stand here all night?"

I turn obediently and follow him. He walks slightly ahead, his hands jammed into the mufflike pockets of his jacket. Strange, I think, that he seems so angry. At school he is always so mild.

"I wasn't all that late," he says, still sulky.

"No," I say gently, "I know."

"I couldn't get out of the goddam store. Adamiewicz, the old guy who runs the place, has this kidney business he's got to tell me all about. And then right at nine when we're supposed to close, this slob come in with a big order, they're having a party."

"What kind of store is it?" I ask.

"Grocery. I'm the only guy he's got there, see. I mean, he used to do a good business and when my brother worked there, there were two other guys. Butcher and another clerk. Then they built the Grand Union over on Claremont Avenue. Hey."

He says this with a thrust of his head, to direct my attention to something, and he kicks, proudly, the tire of the car I had seen him driving before. I look at him, perplexed.

"It's mine now," he says. "All mine."

"Wasn't it always?"

"Nah, it belonged to my brother. He went into the Army last week."

"I didn't know you had a brother."

"Yeah, well, he hasn't lived in Clifton for a while. He rented a room in Twin Falls where he worked. He worked nights a lot and didn't like coming home. Now, though, he's someplace in New Jersey. Fort Dix, I guess. It runs okay. Kicks a little. You want to go on in?" He's talking about Patty's, not the car, and I look at the house, dark from the street, and then without really thinking about alternatives, say, "No, let's not." He looks at me, then reaches over and opens the car door for me and there's nothing to do but get in.

He doesn't drive at all fast, just loves the car along. He makes the turn onto Hill and then drives straight up and out, north, past the turn-off to the golf course, past the horse farm where for years Houghtons used to raise and breed race horses, but now, only an occasional stud nickers in the foaming grass, and past the horse cemetery, five or six rows of short granite slabs marking the carcasses of once-famed horseflesh. Past the old house built way out here in God knows when or why, all leaning turrets, towers, sagging porches, punched-out windows, a shell for the wind to whistle through, and Hendricks Dairy where an overblown cow stares placidly into our headlights—her giant teats remind me uneasily of the burden of womanhood we share —and on to a drive-in, J*O*H*N*N*Y'S, a hamburger place I've passed a million times on this road and never squandered a look at, my mother so squeamish I was never even allowed to buy popcorn at Woolworth's, much less did we dine at anything like this. Stephen drives into the empty graveled lot and honks. There is no one else, no other customers. He honks again. A man comes out and Stephen rolls down the window.

"Oh, hi ya, Steve," the man says, "how ya doin', anyhow?"

"All right, John," Stephen says. "Nobody out tonight, huh?"

"Hell no," John says. "Never nobody out once it gets cool. And the movie's dead until spring. Cost me more to operate this here sign than I make in a day."

Johnny does look poor. In the neon white of the sign his skin is orchid-gray, his lips a chilled violet. He is not a young man, and his peaked white cap sits foolishly on his hair. Stephen orders two hamburgers and two Cokes and when John clamps the tray onto the window he makes a display over the food. I like him for this and John looks pleased. Stephen is anyway very hungry. He eats the first burger in four bites.

"I used to come out here with my brother when he was living home. Two or three nights a week we'd eat out here." He laughs and says, "You'd like my brother. He's kind of a crazy guy."

"Like you?" I say.

He starts on the second hamburger and says, "No, what I mean is, he's really smart. He's got brains. Pete can tell you almost anything you want to know about an engine. You hear a little knock in the front, and you think, now what the hell's coming off here, and Pete'll say, geez, there's that number two cylinder not firing right. He's got more ideas on how to fix things than anybody I ever knew."

"What kind of work does he do?"

Stephen shrugs. "Ah, I don't know. He's a mechanic down at the big GM plant in Twin Falls. Hell, he makes good pay and all, but all he does, he says, he walks around with this little wrench and gives things a twitch. He knew the whole floor cold in a week. I want him to quit and get some more school in."

"You mean go to college?" I ask.

"He never even finished high school. My old man, that bastard, made him quit."

This casual hatred shocks me. I look into the blue-brown of my Coke and shake the shaved ice.

"But you're going to college, aren't you?" I ask. He is in the straight academic section with me, and all of the boys in it go to college. "You could probably get a basketball scholarship."

"Me?" He wipes his fingers on the little white paper napkin and, balling it, tosses it out of the car window. It bounces over the dark gravel, rolling to rest near Johnny's empty wire trash basket. I want, for a moment, to get out of the car and drop it in. "I'll be lucky if I make it through high school."

"But why?" I say. "I heard Mrs. Moran tell Binky that you're the best mathematician the school has had in years."

"Geez, math isn't anything. It's just a game. I like to fool around with it, that's all. I don't get Latin much. And English, uh."

"You don't study," I say primly.

"Yeah," he agrees. "Though history's okay this year, and chem is good."

"Oh," I say, "do you think so? Reduction of iron ore, now really."

"Well, hell," he says, "it's good to know that stuff. Hey, have a bite of this, huh? I'll bet you don't eat anything, do you? What happened, you used to be kind of fat."

"I lost weight," I say stiffly, ignoring the crimped paper plate he is holding out to me.

"Though you didn't look so bad fat. You're getting too skinny now. I'll bet they don't even have to X-ray you, just hold you up to a strong light."

I smile and with this encouragement take a bit of the hamburger. It's awful, ground cardboard. I wonder how he can stand to eat it. I give it back to him to finish and he does, then lights a cigarette and one for me. He laughs as I smoke it. Why, I ask him, but he won't tell me why. We sit smoking and then he turns and puts his arm up on the back of the seat. His hand is only an inch or two from my face.

"You always take off like you did tonight?"

"The party was boring," I say, "that's why. And I'm not a very good waiter. I hate to be bored. I could think of lots of things to do better than sitting there."

"Like what?" he asks. Carefully, his fingers move from the ridge of the car seat cover to the shoulder seam of my coat. Clear through an inch of wool I feel the weight of his hand, and it makes me nervous.

"I don't know," I say, and then, suddenly reckless, decide to tell the truth. "I read a lot." Surprisingly, this does not seem to shock him.

"Yeah? What do you read? Movie magazines? That's what my stepmother reads. Then lunchtime in the cafeteria you see all the girls reading those love comics."

"No," I say, "I don't read those."

"What's the matter," he asks. "You got something against love?"

Now, in a tumble, all the things I have heard about him come back to me. Newsreel-like, his other clinches flutter behind my eyelids and I am frozen, momentarily a spectator at my own folly. Where is the door? The door handle? But he is smiling.

"And I thought all you girls wanted was to get married."

Now we are safe, away from love. "That's all girls," I say. "I don't want that."

"What do you want to do?"

I take a breath. What can I tell him? Of my philosophic dreams? My spacious clean sunny house, the garden which I work at sunrise, and then my day: so many hours for music, so many for botany, bugs, art, history and literature, and appearing now and then when I recess, delightful golden-haired children. But no husband. At lease not regularly. Or a very rich one who is busy. Why elect tyranny? He looks at me waiting and I twist the button of my coat. "It's all because I hate being bored. I don't know why it is but most women—the married ones I mean, the ones my mother's age, they're all so tired or unhappy or bored or they want to live your life for you. Do you know what I mean? Well, I don't want to be that way. I don't want to end up like that. There's so much to do if you have the freedom. Why get married? Why spoil it?" He is quiet, and I think well, that fixed it, that's that, but then he laughs and starts the car. I look at him and he looks at me and shakes his head.

"You're a real crazy girl," he says. We ride down the long hills into town. He drives happily, I can tell, and fast, and to make it better, we slide under all the green lights, as if the gates of the city were one by one opening for us and we ride straight down Hill Street and he makes the turn and stops in front of my house.

"That was some swell party you asked me to," he says.

"I'm sorry," I say, "we could have gone in."

"Nah," he says, "I don't know those kids too well anyhow. I don't hang with that crowd. Maybe if you want to we could go out some other time."

"All right," I say.

"Would you," he says, and I see he is looking at me in a very worried way and then he licks his lips and his head drops down. After all I have heard, I am unprepared and I don't have time to close my eyes. Our lashes tangle, his nose bumps mine, crosses it, adjusts, and I am surprised, finally, by his mouth. He stops, and puts his arm firmly around me. Eyes shut, we kiss again. I have a blind sense of texture, his mouth hard on mine, the roughness of his chin. His heart thuds under my hand. When he stops I push away, breathe good night, open the door, and run up the steps of our house. In the dark living room I go to the window. His car, a slick black whale, is still sitting under the street lamp and as I watch, it slowly moves away. In the kitchen my father's tea kettle whistles. My mother's room is dark. I go to the third floor without putting on any lights, and undress quickly and get into my bed. I lie awake for a long time, straight as a line on the cold sheet, as tense and silently alive as a lightly brushed string.

6

In work clothes—paint-daubed coveralls—Schaeffer sits in our kitchen having coffee. As he lifts the cup his face heats pleasure, his thin lips pucker—too hot? He sips and smiles, widely.

"Miz Munson, you make a good cup of coffee."

He is relaxed, with the loose ease of a large dog. To me, used to seeing my father's alert compactness on that chair, this man looks like disorganization.

Four is my mother's coffee hour. She makes two pots of coffee every day, one for breakfast—hot and strong at eight, lukewarm for lunch—a new pot now which she will pour out until bedtime. The nine-thirty cup is always cold, bitter, the milk in it marbling. With coffee, she eats bread. Bread is the staff of her life.

Upstairs on the third floor, in my cleared-out room, the workmen have left their traces: a barrelful of plaster chips, finger-printed walls. Everywhere on the third floor, a sour snow of plaster dust has fallen and even here, in the kitchen I can smell it.

"Why, thank you," my mother says, quite gaily. She hooks a strand of hair behind her ear, slides the coffee pot onto an asbestos pad, and sits down at the table. "My daughter tells me I'm a terrible cook, but I have no incentive, Mr. Schaeffer. None. Dr. Munson has a bad stomach and can't eat ordinary food, and Eleanor! Well, look at her. She doesn't eat a thing, not a thing. Girls these days all want to be scarecrows."

I grin and pour myself a cup of coffee, then edge away, into the dining room. Homework. There on the table my stained and blotted books. I push the lace tablecloth back to make a work area. Sit down, open book, look, no, sip coffee first, too hot. Wait. He didn't say anything to me today. Didn't even look. Leapt up at the bell—scowled—went out back door. Lost in jingling tide. I cool, calm, collected papers, self, waited for crowd to thin before I elbowed in. At sill of sea, Coleman calls from tipping shut the top windows with the blackboard pointer. Miss Munson, I'd like to talk to you about your math. Well what? What is there to say? And later in the cream-colored basement cafeteria, below the churn and clank of large pipes, I watch starving pinch-faced students line up for food served by bloated women in white with meaty arms who scoop the stuff onto tin trays—splish-splat, dring—cash register rings, students shuffle forward as patiently as animals for their chow. I nurse a nickel Coke rinsing it through my teeth to make it last longer. Across from me Patty eats and eats, two ham-lettuce-tomato sandwiches, a pickle, a slab of spice cake, and drinks milk, at least a quart. I stare over the black spring of her hair into the boys' side of the cafeteria. My view of Stephen's back is unimpeded. He sits with two other members of the basketball team and they laugh. Hilariously. Their laughter makes me nervous. His eyes, in math class, were frosty, as if the ski sweater he wears today—a pale blue with ribbons of crystals—had turned him into a frozen Nordic god. And why is he laughing now?

Dear dead wife!

"Did you know Alice, Miz Munson?"

All dead, all dead. The youngest of five, all dead. Mother died young, yours too? Mine heart, yours too? Rheumatic heart, big killer, then as now. Wife died cancer, One breast, two, four years, then gone. Suffered. Hard to bear suffering of those you love. Easier, maybe, to bear own. Thirty happy years, no children, no dogs, never left Clifton beyond Fullerton, except summers to fish at the lake. Up there all summer, little white house, kerosene stove, candles, birches right down to the water. Say. You like fish?

Frieda?

My father yells up front stairs. Passing me he inquires, your mother there? I point with pen. Frieda? Oh, hello.

Schaeffer, stork-legged, half rises, I see from my chair how knees of coverall buckle.

Sit down, sit down, just looking for a bottle of phenobarbital. I don't suppose you've seen it, Frieda? I left it here this morning.

Mother sighs, rises. His Woman must look for His Things. The top of the kitchen cupboard full of medicines in brown bottles, green bottles, clear bottles, boxes full of sample pills in little cardboard folders.

Are you sure you left it up here, Fred?

The telephone!

I jump, coffee sloshes. Hot brown blot melts blue ruled line on paper. I rise, run to living room where sleek black messenger sings on small square tottery wooden table. As I lift receiver the table trembles: Yes. It is. He. He is going, reluctantly, it seems, to drive to the next city. For his old man. A big pain. Will I go?

Thinking yes but have to ask first. Down receiver, hurry past place where virgin paper gathers only coffee-pox, into kitchen where father, now sitting in mother's chair, explains excitedly to pained Schaeffer the causes of car-cin-o-gen-a-tion while mother grumbles and clinks, seeking father's philo-phelo-pheno.

Who with, she wants to know. Losing courage, must go, lie.

Patty.

Liar. Patty calls? A risk. All life a risk. Fly, dive or swim, ride in car with strange boy all alone to strange town, strange place and back before nine.

Oh yes, all right. Grumble, clink. Yes.

What's that, father asks, looking up. Where's she going? Rush past him, past brown-stained brackish books, to tottery table, fondle sleek messenger, breathe sweetly in its warm and waiting pores, all right. I will. Yes.

"I told him no, I'm not gonna go anymore, what the hell, driving all the way there to do his dirty jobs. Let him do it himself." Stephen has come to pick me up, and we have first to go back to his place where he must wait for his father. He drives up Hill Street, swooping angrily under orange lights.

"Do what?" I ask. "What is it you're going to do?"

Behind us, a pug-faced bread truck screeches, then honks.

"Lot of, excuse me, shit. I'm sorry, Ellie, I just got a lot to do tonight and I got a long practice tomorrow. Wanted to fool around with the math some before the test Wednesday." The test, for which I have been studying off and on for two weeks, is the midterm. When I think about it, a small tic begins to go in my stomach and my palms grow cold. We swoop up the hill, this whale has wings, then go east, down a hill and east again. We edge past Houghton's parking field where cars, mostly new and all colors, are parked as carefully as scarabs. We pass the mill itself, caught in a net of wire fencing. The old mill, of a dull pleasant brick, looks like a school. From its central tower, a blue E used to fly during the war. The newer buildings, new-brick pink, are beginning now to disgorge men. The lights of the mill go on, all at once, as if specifically for our eyes. Even in this closed car, through the mill's windows I can hear the chunk-a-chunk-a-chunk of the looms. We turn a corner and Stephen parks. The hill is very steep here, and Stephen's house, one of a block of dirty gray stone, seems sunk into the earth as if embedded against erosion. The house is narrow, squeezed, and down four stone steps is the front door. He shoves it open. We enter a stingy hall which is lit by a small yellow bulb and smells of cauliflower. Next into a dark room—oddly, the shades are drawn—and in this gloaming I make out a sofa, a television set on a stand, and absorbing the central space, a large round table. Past this, a well-lit doorway frames a pair of polished black shoes that are crossed and propped on a chair.

"That you, Steve?"

"Yeah," Stephen, in front of me, leans on the doorjamb and talks to the feet. "Where's the stuff?"

"Upstairs. Floor of my closet. Who's that?"

"Nobody you know. I'll be right back," he says to me over his shoulder. "Don't go away."

Stephen's father is sitting at the wooden kitchen table paring an apple.

"Hello," I say. "I'm Eleanor Munson."

"Hi," he says, and pulls out the chair on the other side of his feet. "Wanna sit?" Obediently, I go around the table and sit down. Next to the coiled pile of apple peels is a bottle of Budweiser.

"You Steve's girlfriend?" he asks, munching and looking at me sharply from under a sharp gray felt.

"I'm not sure yet," I say. "I don't know Stephen very well."

"Just a friend, ha?" he says, and laughs. He is well dressed—white shirt, navy-blue trousers, red- and blue-striped tie—all pressed, and a big chest swelling out his shirt buttons. Big shoulders. Tough face, square bones in it are hard and round. Short, blunt nose, small blue eyes. Not a bit like Stephen. He pops a chunk of carved apple into his mouth and chews, then cuts another chunk and offers it, clasped between thumb and knife blade, to me. I refuse. He shrugs.

"Apple a day keeps the doctor away."

"I've had mine, thanks," I say, hoping it sounds amiable, but it comes out cold and too hoity-toity.

"Where you from? Around here?"

"You mean Clifton?"

"I mean, from around Cassell Street, Polack Hill. No, huh? You don't look like it. You from Hill Street section?"

"I live downtown," I say.

"Yeah?" His eyes, which are studying me, do not seem satisfied. I feel my face begin to shine and wish suddenly I had streak-bleached hair and a tight see-through sweater on. To relieve the pressure of his glare I look around the kitchen. The cabinets are tan and need cleaning. There is no curtain at the back window and a glazed row of milk bottles marches across the sill. There is a large refrigerator and, looking as if it had no place to go, a dishwasher, more or less in the middle of the floor, though in the sink I can see a stack of used dishes.

"Hey!" Steve's father shouts up to a corner over my head. "Steve! Wrap it up, will you? There's a paper up there somewhere." Over my head I hear Stephen's steps, the creak of the floor boards.

The apple is finished, core and all, and Stephen's father drinks his beer.

"What's your father do?" he asks me. This makes me blush.

"He's a doctor," I say.

"Yeah?" Unlike the rest of Clifton he is unimpressed. Does he think I'm lying? "What'd you say your name was?"

From outside, on the stone steps, I hear the click of sharp female heels. The door opens, its glass panel rattles, the door slams closed and rattles again.

"For the love of—hey, Mike?" Papers rustle. Now I hear one heel only. Packages are dumped on the living-room table and a woman comes hopping to the kitchen door. She bends, clutches the heel of a black suede spike, and takes it off. "You know what I just did on the friggin' doormat? Oh, hi." She looks at me carelessly, then hops across the doorsill, broken shoe in hand. She has on a shiny black leather coat and seems very tall. She puts a hand on the corner of Mike's chair and drops the shoe on the table. "Cheap things," she says to him. "How do you like that? I just bought the goddam things last week. You Steve's girl?"

"Or something like that," Mike says.

"Like what?" she asks, and gives me a big flashing smile.

Confused but trying to be honest, I smile back. "I'm not anything yet."

"Never mind, hon," she says, "you'll get there. What am I gonna do with these damn shoes, Mike," she asks him, pouting.

"Toss 'em," he says. He picks up the shoe and pitches it across the room toward a full bag of garbage leaning in risky equipoise. Luckily, the shot is short.

"Stop showing off, will ya?" she says, shrugging out of the shiny coat and kicking off the second shoe. She throws the coat into the living room where it lands, sprawling, like something recently shot, on the sofa. The shoe follows it. She's tall, with big hips and a deep low bosom and a neat waist. I guess she must be around thirty, but she looks younger because of a shake of freckles across her nose.

"Where you been all day?" Mike says to her. "I called you at one."

"Here we go again," she says to me, "the big quiz. You'd think there was that much to do in this town. I was out, kiddo," she says to him, "shopping." She reaches out her arm and plucks the hat from his head and kisses his bald forehead. He grabs her wrist and gets the hat back and she laughs and goes out to the living room. Snap and the TV is on.

"I bought some undies for your son," she yells. "The big dope is running around in shreds."

"Let him buy his own undies," Mike says. Upstairs, the floor to the left of my head creaks, the staircase shakes echoing thuds, and Stephen comes down carrying a bundle wrapped in newspaper under his arm.

"The boy himself," the woman says.

"Okay," Stephen says to me from the living room, "let's go."

"Hey, Steve," the woman says, coming up behind him, "I got you the cutest new shorts. I had them embroider on your initial."

"Swell," he says, not looking at her and jerking his head at me. I get up and smile at his father, a big bland smile.

"It was very nice meeting you, Mr. Wojcik."

He grunts.

I squeeze out the narrow doorway to the living room. The TV is soundless and flashing a blizzard of flecks. Rosemary is leaning on one hand and, can-stuck-out, is hitting the set with the flat of the other. We press past her and Stephen says, "Cut it out you're going to break it."

"What's the matter, don't they teach you anything in school? Can't you fix this thing?"

"Fix it yourself," he says.

"Hey, kid," Mike says from the doorway, and I am surprised to see that he is quite short, shorter than Rosemary, much shorter than Stephen, "watch your mouth and tell Smitty I'll be by next week."

"Yeah, yeah," says Stephen. He grabs my arm and pulls me out after him, into the sallow air of the hall, out the dark entry, up the steps. Opposite us Houghton's has blacked out. Only the lights of the main buildings are on. Above us the anemic fluorescent street lamp shines, coloring us blue.

"Sonofabitch," Stephen says bitterly. We get into the car and it is a long time before he says anything else.

The drive down and out of town is long, dark, and tense, but after we get on Route 5 things are better. He drives fast. I feel the thrust of his anger melt in the speed we are pushing, energy smashed again into speed. The dark we are driving into brings peace; night and speed heal all. In our headlights billboards loom up and by. Cover the Earth, Fisk. Next to us the railroad tracks crosshatch an eastward pattern, next to the railroad the river negligently races the tracks and across the river, up the other bank on 5-a other cars parallel our drive.

Ten miles out of town he says, "That Rosemary, she gets me, she really does."

"Does she really buy your underwear?" I ask, timid again.

"Why not?" he says. "She's got all the dough. I can't get a cent out of the old man. I either get it from her or nobody and I'll be goddamned if I'll ask her for money." He glances at me and then says, "See, she's not my real mother. Well, hell, you know that. My mother's dead, she died when I was eight. She was Bill Flipman's mother's sister. She was to Rosemary like night is to day, I mean, she was a real old-fashioned mother, you know? Cleaned the house and cooked good food. She learned how to cook Polish food for my father. Pirozhki. You ever had pirozhki? They're these little dough things with meat inside. She was very religious, see, even though she wasn't born a Catholic. She turned Catholic when they got married. The trouble was, she used to take everything. She cried all the time. My father knocked her around a lot and she never would say anything. He's never laid a hand on Rosemary, though. It's something you can't figure out." He squints ahead on a turn then passes the logy, putting dump truck in front of us. "Your brother got killed in the war, didn't he?"

Did he? What is there for me to say that's simple?

"Yes," I say.

"That must have been hard for your folks. He was pretty smart, wasn't he?"

"I guess so. Who told you?"

"One of the guys, I don't remember who. Supposed to go to some big-name college, wasn't he?"

"Yes," I say. "He enlisted, though. We all thought he was too young. He was seventeen. My father gave his consent. I think it's stupid to enlist like that. If you had a chance to now, would you enlist?"

He thinks this over. "Yeah," he says, "I would. It's just as good as hanging around Clifton."

"What's the matter, don't you like being alive?"

"Somebody's got to fight," he offers. "Anyway, there are things you can't help, like the government. Suppose they send me a letter saying, okay, buddy, you're in. What am I supposed to do? Say no?"

"You could."

"Sure, and spend twice the time in the clink. You know something, you're not very practical."

I look out the side window, at the black scenery streaming by. "You know what I think? Better clink than nothing. Suppose everyone just refused to fight? That would end it. Absolute rebellion. But people won't do it. They're afraid of what other people think, more afraid of that than death. Or else they don't believe they're going to die. They know it but don't believe it."

He laughs. "I believe it. Un-immortal me. Stephen Wojcik, common clay."

"You're funny. You really have no ego at all, do you? Aren't you proud of the things you do well?"

"Like what? Name them. Name three."

I think and name one, math, and two, basketball, and he

laughs when I hesitate. "You did leave out one," he says. "The basic one." In the dark his hand reaches over the neutral space inspired by the stick shift. Amiably, he squeezes my knee.

We drive through Riverton, the little town before Twin Falls, and then approach the bridge. The long up-curved bridge is lit by old lamps, round globes set firmly on frilled iron stalks. The cool blue breath of the river rises to meet the warmth of these lamps, creates for each one a misty halo which, disbursed by our speed, becomes an amber haze. The bridge flees behind us, an orange rainbow. Ahead is the phosphorescent green of downtown. Higher buildings, wider streets, brighter lights. Shoppers hurry in and out of stores. Things never close down here. I gape, a true Clifton hick. Stephen, though, turns to a dingier prospect, a cramped street of wooden houses where posters peel and flap on deserted store fronts and some of the doorways are boarded over. Loiterers, bums, adolescents, stand in front of a bar. There is no other sign of life. He stops at the only other light on the street, a candy store. In the dirty, dimly lit window is a Coke-drinking cardboard girl. The teeth in her wide smile are pocked with flyspecks. Stephen turns and with a long stretch gets the bundle from the back seat.

"Right back," he says, getting out. I see him cross the car in front of me. He looks stern. He scuffs up the single step and shoves through the door. A bell tinkles. The door slams behind him. I worry. Suppose he doesn't come back? But the door opens, tinkling, and Stephen slams it hard. Crossing in front of me he looks happier, opening the door, he smiles. "Hey," he says, "where do you want to eat?"

. . . . .

We eat in a cafeteria on Front Street that is like the school cafeteria but worse: sanitary tile walls, dirty black-and-white tile floors. Every table is occupied by an old lady with a shopping bag (what do they carry in them, you wonder) or a shaky, shabby-coated old man. We go together to get the food—mashed potatoes, meat loaf with tomato sauce, and creamed corn, scooped out of the stainless steel bin by a red-faced giant who booms "There you go kids" as he plops this on plates. We slide our trays past piles of rolls, doughnuts, layer cakes, and a case full of jewel-colored Jellos. Stephen takes Jello, and chocolate pie, and a container of milk, and I get coffee. We eat at a table for two pushed against the wall. Stephen distributes our plates and lays the empty trays on the table next to us. He eats using his left hand but keeps his right arm on the table too.

"Not bad," he says, shoveling up a forkful of potato. He points with his fork to the food. "Why'ent you eat?"

The reason I don't is that my fork has lipstick on it, not my color, but I don't want to tell him about this, so I say, "I will, I'm just resting. I was scared waiting for you."

"You were?" he says. "Why? Nothing was going to happen."

"I didn't know that. What a creepy street. Anything could have."

"I'm not going to do it again. Go on, eat, will you. I hate to buy food for a girl and then have her not eat it."

"Do you buy food for lots of girls?"

"Huh? Oh, once in a while. I used to take out Nora Novak a lot. You know her?"

I shake my head. He looks relieved.

"She's a good kid. She goes to St. Stan's. Try the meat anyway. You know, Rosie's not a bad cook but she doesn't cook much. They go out a lot. My father's got a lot of business here and in Albany."

"What does he do?" I ask.

Stephen butters a piece of roll with short, neat strokes. "He's a gambler."

"He is?" I say, awed. "All the time?"

"Yeah. He could make a lot, you know? The trouble is, he bets himself. That way, he comes out about even. Doesn't fool with the numbers, just horses. You ever been out to Saratoga?"

I shake my head.

"We'll go in the summer," he says. "My brother and I used to go. I've been every year since I was twelve. You have to be sixteen but I was always a tall kid after I got to be twelve-thirteen. I like the horses myself, but the way I figure it is, if you bet to place then you never really lose. You never make it either, but who does? My brother Pete, though, he's always getting in over his head. Doesn't know where to stop, like with Rosemary too." He looks up at me and then down again. "Now, why the hell did I say that?" he asks his plate.

He has his Jello, and the chocolate pie, and then decides to get some coffee. Drinking it, he says, "I shouldn't have said that about Rosemary. I don't know, she got me with that underwear business. What a bird-brain. And I can't get a nickel from him. After my mother died the old man brought *her* home. For us, he says, because we need a woman in the house. So there she is all day, eating, sleeping, filling up the house with her junk. The bathroom's always *occupado* and the TV's going all day. So Pete says to my father, Hey, Pop, it doesn't look good, you know? We got this kid here—me, he means—and here's this dame lying around in plain daylight. So they get married. That idiot, my brother. Next thing you know she's out shopping every day. That's all that bird-brain does is shop. In between, she's giving my brother the big eye. Well, see, she's not that old. She's—what am I, seventeen?—Pete's twenty-two now, she's maybe twenty-six. That's old, but not that old, you follow me? And Pete's so goddamned stupid he's taking it where it's put out. Damn it, excuse me."

But my look is more of awe than embarrassment. It's all so fascinating, and I'm the kind of girl who's always wanted to spend a week in a whorehouse to see how the other half lives. "What happened then?" I ask. "Did your father find out Rosemary was—flirting?"

"Flirting?" he says. He gives me a blank look and then starts to laugh. "Oh Christ, Ellie," he says and shakes his head at me, laughing. "I don't know what I'm shooting my mouth off at you for."

"Is that why your brother left? I mean, why he went to live in Twin Falls?"

He finishes his pie and pushes the plate away. "What? Oh, yeah. One day my father says to me, Hey Stevie, anybody you know been warming up my side of the bed?

Huh? I say, real surprised. Go on, Pop, you got rocks in your head. He makes a little joke which I won't pass on to you—flirting, Christ—and I go up to my brother's room and pack his flight bag. You know something? That idiot didn't want to go? Rather stay home and get his throat cut. What a stupid bastard."

At the table next to us, an old man who has been struggling with his food finally does spill his tea all over himself, the table and the floor. He gets up from the table shaking badly and holding on to the table's edge. We help him mop it up with napkins and one of the busboys comes over and says to him, "Now, that's all right, mister, now, don't feel bad," but the man, who is neatly dressed, seems worried about the coat. Stephen tells him it will clean right out, but the man keeps shaking his head and mumbling and rubbing at the wet spot with skinny fingers. We leave and walk down the block to where the car is parked. Stephen takes my hand. In the car we sit very close to each other, my left side locked to his right, and after we get out of the downtown traffic he puts his arm around me. The trouble with the car is, it's got a stick shift and whenever we slow down he has to untangle. Halfway home, something, a chipmunk or squirrel, whizzes out of the woods and stands stupefied in our lights for that moment before we thud over it.

"Oh Christ, no," Stephen says. I feel my own stomach go sour. "Damn animals don't have sense enough to keep off the road." He looks anxiously into the rear-view mirror, but behind us there's nothing but the bright, burrowing eyes of a car moving up in back. "I hate to do that," he says. "It's bad luck. I'll have bad luck for a week, louse up the math, and won't play worth a nickel at practice. You want to come?"

"To what? The practice?"

"Yeah. I can fix it if you want to. The other guys' girls all come. Okay?"

He drops me in front of the house at 8:31 by the YMCA clock. And kisses me. This time it's better, I'm more prepared. Still, it's too early. From upstairs, our second floor, the lit windows frown down on my dalliance. Any moment, I think, my mother may lift the curtain, or my father come bumbling out on one of his evening trips to the drug store. The lights are still too bright. Love, not heliotropic, flourishes in the dark. His mouth covers mine again, and I push, gently, against his bunched heart, covered by his jacket and the stiff felt letter C.

"I'm sorry about all the yakking I did," he says.

"That's all right," I say. "You didn't say anything wrong."

"All my life I've been kind of a silent type, stuck to myself pretty much, except for my brother. I don't know why I talk so much to you. I keep telling myself, shut up."

His face, angled down at me, is a faint worried violet. "I don't know, I guess I'm kind of nuts. I'm worried about my brother, see. I wouldn't care, but the jerk can't take care of himself and they're sending him to Korea. At least, I guess that's where it is." He digs in his pants pocket and comes up with a crumpled blue envelope, and then squashes it back. "Hell," he says.

118

The YMCA clock jerks to 8:41. "I've got to go," I say. "I told my mother I was going to Patty's."

"You did," he says frowning. "What for?"

"I don't know," I say. "She's strict."

"You'd better tell her from now on."

He is sitting on the edge of the seat looking down at me. I have a clear view of the outline of his face—the long flat cheek, the sharp angle of his chin and the length of his neck. From our last kiss I remember that his chin is rough and his neck smooth and warm, and I want to touch him there under his chin where estrogen and androgen meet. I reach out and put two fingers there, then I laugh and get out of the car. At the sidewalk I blow him a kiss and he still looks startled. I run up the steps of our house. At the door I meet my father, baggy-pocketed, going out. He seems not to recognize me as I run past him through the door.

7

It is Thanksgiving Day and we are feeding Schaeffer. In the dining room my mother pulls the drapes against the dull sky. The candles are lit. They flicker, then soar, feeding on air, give the damasked table, the silverware, our faces, a fluttering vermeil sheen. The food is brought in ceremoniously, dish after dish, and at last, the turkey, a polished mahogany giant, is wheeled on a serving cart to my father's side.

I sit between my father and mother, and across from me sits our guest. He watches, with an expression both curious and nauseated, like someone watching a bad accident, as my father carves. I avert my eyes. Poor dead bird. My father, no carver, slashes and rips at the peaked glossy chest that I had tended so carefully all morning. He balances a chunk of white meat between carving knife and fork and drops it on the platter. His look is cheerful.

"I never did like carving," he remarks and sits down to serve the plates stacked in front of him.

"Heavens!" my mother exclaims as the plates go around. "I forgot the wine." She jumps to get the decanter from the sideboard and begins to fill our glasses with decanted Virginia Dare. My father has begun to eat, and my mother, pouring Schaeffer's glass, sees that my father has passed him a blank plate.

"Why, Fred," she says, "you haven't given Mr. Schaeffer anything."

My father looks up, amazed. The candles on the table make yellow flashes like exclamation marks on his spectacles. "I haven't!" he says. "Can you beat that? Getting older and blinder every year." My mother puts the decanter down and begins, herself, to ladle Schaeffer's plate full.

"String beans?" she inquires. "Stuffing?"

He looks up at her with a timid, grateful, puppyish look. "Yes, thank you. It's been a long time since I've had anyone's cooking but my own, and that's not much."

Today he has on a light-gray double-breasted suit with wide lapels, a white shirt, and a yellow tie. Something about the suit, its slack generosity of cut, makes him look like a man in borrowed clothes. The suit fits him coldly, like an armor. He seems to shrink from contact with it, as if the sides were unfamiliar steel.

With a sigh my mother sits down and looks around the table, checking again. She picks up her fork. My father, unaware that we haven't yet started, has nearly gone through his helpings, like ours but puréed. "Oh!" my mother says, and puts her fork down again. "You'll have to forgive us, Mr. Schaeffer. I suppose you're used to a prayer of some kind. Eleanor used to say our prayers, but she's grown too intellectual. Do you have one you'd like to repeat?"

Schaeffer clears his throat, screws his eyes shut, and ducks his head. I drop my head in token politeness. By rotating my eyes one hundred eighty degrees to the left I discern my father picking his nose. Over in the other corner my mother is frowning and by contortions of facial expression trying to attract his attention.

"And so, dear Lord," Schaeffer says, "let us all give thanks for Thy plenty." We mumble amen and my father, who has been caught by my mother's eye, wipes his hands briskly on the napkin.

"Very nice," my mother comments bitterly but smiles at Schaeffer, and we begin to eat. My father's plate is clean and this distresses me, for it means that the dull part of dinner is over. My father's frayed eyebrows are peaked in interest, there is a conversational glitter in the rounds of his lenses. He lifts his fork and lets it drop as if it were a reflex hammer, all the while studying Schaeffer.

"Are you a Protestant, Schaeffer?" my father inquires.

Addressed, Schaeffer swallows hastily and wipes his lips with the napkin. "A Methodist, sir, a Methodist."

My mother sighs and gives me a helpless look. "Fred, why don't you let Mr. Schaeffer eat his dinner? We can talk later on."

"Oh," my father says, "am I annoying you, Schaeffer?"

"No, no," Schaeffer protests, "not at all. I was about to say that I used to be more active in church affairs. While my wife was alive. After she passed away I didn't go in quite as regular."

"Ahh," my father says, "the ladies. I'm not sure whether religion was invented for them or by them."

My mother makes a noise in her throat, and Schaeffer

says hurriedly, "Now, I didn't mean anything like that. It's just that when Alice passed away—"

"Our tenant-to-be," my father interrupts, "will quite probably be female. And Catholic."

"Very possibly," my mother says, "since you have ruled against the male sex. Mr. Schaeffer! Have some cranberry sauce, please. It's right there at your elbow."

"Why—uh—thank you, Miz Munson. Nothing goes better with turkey than cranberry sauce. Now, you won't believe this but my grandfather used to —"

"Undoubtedly," my father says, "this female will arise every morning at five to attend confession."

"They don't go to confession that often, Daddy," I put in. "The rule of the Church makes it absolutely necessary once a year. I know lots of Catholics who don't go very often."

"Really! Now, I find that interesting. Is there a youth movement against confession? But what about these eternal novenas? At any rate, I'm quite sure that this lady will slam out of the front door early in the morning to wake the heathen from their sound slumber. Not that I'm against confession. Not at all. I must say that as an instrument of catharsis it's a proven therapeutic agent, rather like the diaries neurotics keep.

"No. As a fact, I'm not at all against it. Or Catholicism. It makes supportable what would otherwise not be. As does any religion. No, I think religion can be a positive good. Although in my opinion it has, thus far, been more of a positive evil. The horrors of the Middle Ages, the Inquisition, the Wars of Religion. All in the name of God. And, of course, the Church, I mean here, The One True Church," he smiles at us all.

"You must excuse my husband, Mr. Schaeffer," my mother puts in now. "He has his own ideas."

"The one true Church," my father goes on, "has done enormous good. In the past. What I do not like about the Catholic Church is that it preys on maiden ladies"—I sense the pun coming and groan, but my father, with a pleased expression, continues—"just as maiden ladies pray in it."

Schaeffer now looks uncomfortably from my mother to my father. Indeed, it is difficult to follow my father's long, brambly rambles through religion, and his route becomes riskier whenever it crosses my mother's. Often, my parents seem to me like competing scout leaders, bent on hacking independent trails up a mountain. Their paths wind, and I, poor lone scout, am always left panting at the last set of blazes, trying to choose. Today, however, I have a troop-mate. Naïvely, Schaeffer volunteers, "I guess there just isn't much else for a single lady to do in Clifton."

"That's it!" my father exclaims. "Carpenter, you've hit the nail on the head. I say: the Catholic Church would fall on its face today were it not supported by the scrawny backs of menopausal females. I'll bet you, Schaeffer, that any Sunday you go into St. Vincent's you'll find: fifty per cent single maiden ladies, twenty per cent young girls under sixteen, ten per cent boys under ten, and that leaves"—he holds up his hand and bends back a finger for each per cent—"uh, twenty per cent—" He thinks and then announces, "Oh yes, the pregnant women. They're most of the young females between eighteen and thirty-eight."

Schaeffer looks serious. "Now, it does seem to me," he says, "that the Catholic families in this town tend toward large size. The last job I did was over on Polack Hill, young feller, couldn'ta been more'n twenty-one-two, had four little ones. Four. Wanted another room put on his place. Now, I ask you, how're those little mouths going to be fed if there's another depression?"

Here my mother brightens. "Now, there's an interesting question," she says. "I sometimes wonder if we must be responsible for *all* those little mouths. If people choose to procreate excessively."

"And do what, Frieda," my father says. "Shall we let them starve? Let the children go hang because of their parents' folly? Nonsense." He pounds the table and the silverware, plates, and glasses jump musically. "No. Let's get at the problem near its root. The Catholic Church is the greatest historical source of superstition, suppression, ignorance, and tyranny. It is coercive in nature, narrow in outlook, materialistic by dedication, and snoopy. It climbs into bed with thousands of married people—"

"Fred—" my mother says.

"It interferes with my medical practice."

"Fred!" my mother says. "For heaven's sake, calm down. Nobody's trying to convert you."

"Why is it," my father asks the air above my mother's head, "that whenever I try to discuss any subject with another intelligent man, you interrupt."

"Because," my mother says, "all your subjects are lectures." This said, she turns bright red, and jumpily serves herself a sweet potato. I apply myself to my own food, waiting. Hot lumps of it slide down my throat, fall to the center of my stomach, and lie in that delicate dark scorching my tender membranes. I sneak a look at Schaeffer. He looks haggard. My father's brilliant lenses have pinned him back against my mother's brick-wall intransigence. I do not look at my father but know exactly what he looks like, how high he is raising his brows, how, in this silence, he is screwing himself up for a terrific artillery of abuse, and then the doorbell rings. We sit paralyzed by the gay little ting-a-ling. My mother laughs, shakily.

"Now, don't tell me!" she says, and hope blooms in her voice like a rose. "That couldn't be a patient. Not on Thanksgiving Day."

I get up and run down the stairs and am stricken to open the door to Stephen.

He was dressed in a suit I'd never seen before and of a kind I'd seen only on John Ritchie, who went away to prep school. It was dark gray and beautifully skimpy and made him look like one stroke of a pen, so bold, tall, thin, and rich looking. I knew he had bought it for me.

"Where'd you get that?" I said. His thin face dilated into a smile.

"You like it? I got it down at Hawthorne's Collegiate."

"You look like a millionaire."

"Who is it, Eleanor?" my mother called from above my head. I turned. Her head, sticking out of the living-room door, seemed lately guillotined and set upon the bannister. "Oh, hello," she said to Stephen. "My, don't you look nice all dressed up. Won't you come in?" One of the things my mother disliked about Stephen was that he was always hanging back, and she called down to me sharply, "Eleanor, don't stand at the door all day letting the heat out," and her head vanished.

"Do you want to come up?" I asked, hoping he would say no. But he wet his lips and tossed the cigarette he was so handsomely holding onto the sidewalk below.

"Well, sure," he said.

"Listen," I whispered. "Before you go upstairs, let me tell you about my father."

"Eleanor!" my mother called. "Please shut the door. There's a draft!"

We went upstairs. As we came in, Schaeffer beamed and stood up.

"Do you want coffee, Fred?" my mother called from the kitchen.

"No!" my father yelled at her.

"What?" she said, coming to the doorway. "Eleanor, don't stand there all day, introduce your friend."

"Stephen Wojcik," I said and Schaeffer's large horny hand shot across the table. My father looked at Stephen, then leaned forward with a hand cupped around his ear.

"What was that?"

"Wojcik," I said.

"Now, how do you spell that?" he asked, frowning.

I pretended not to have heard and propelled Stephen into a chair. We all sat down and ate the pie I had made. It was apple, quite perfect, I thought, so it was disturbing to see my father scrape the pie apples onto his plate and dump the crust into an ashtray. The silence was profound. My mother, to alter its obvious course, asked Schaeffer what he thought of the new mayor, but Schaeffer, now an experienced guest, did not immediately answer.

"Of course," my mother said, "he's a Democrat. All that means to me is high taxes. Milk those who work for those who shirk."

My father smiled, benignly. "You'll have to excuse my wife," he said to Schaeffer. "She doesn't think politics, she feels them."

"Dear God," my mother said bitterly. "You have just spent an hour haranguing us on the influence of Catholicism, and now you say that feeling does not exist in politics."

"Not at all," my father said. "I stated, or rather, implied, that it does but shouldn't. You, Frieda, should think—rather than feel—politics."

"That's absurd, absolutely absurd. You can't separate the two, Fred. Surely you know that. Where does one establish the border line?"

"Muddy thinking! Not enough boundaries! That's what's wrong with the world today, Frieda."

"Let's not branch out, Fred. More pie, anyone?" My mother stood up and began jerking the dessert plates off the table. Stephen, left with a forkful of apple and no plate, looked at me. I shrugged. With a high, surprised sound—a handsaw biting a knot—Schaeffer cleared his throat.

"I wonder," he began, "if anyone would like to go for a drive? A nice drive in the country? If it's not too cold."

My mother turned to look at him over her shoulder. Her eyes were glitter-bright, her voice still shaky. "Why, yes. Yes, why don't we do that. I'd love to see your place at the lake, Mr. Schaeffer. Why don't we drive out there?"

"Out there today?" Schaeffer asked.

"Now," my mother said.

"Yes," Schaeffer said. "Yes, why don't we do that."

"A fine idea," my father said. "The country; peace; quiet."

"Do you want to come, Fred?" my mother said, getting her coat from the closet. "Or do you think it will be too damp for you?"

"Hmm," my father said. "Perhaps I ought to stay home. I've got some work to do. No holidays in this business."

We got on our coats, went down and Out. I had expected to see the weathered pickup truck, but instead a wide green Buick was parked as carefully as an emerald at our curb. With a gesture noble and bold, Schaeffer laid his hand to the silver handle, and as if he were boosting my mother into the stirrup propelled her up and in. Just then, a window flew up and my father leaned out.

"Oh, Frieda," he shouted down, "what shall I tell your daughter Sylvia, should she call?"

My mother's red-hatted head popped out of the car

window. "That I'm out," she shouted back. Stephen and I got in the back seat. Schaeffer opened the driver's door and with a look lordly and proud seated himself, adjusted the mirror, grappled with the hand brake. He took the fine-fashioned steering wheel and hunching forward just a little, pressed START. The green steed bucked suddenly, once, and then settled into an even, paced glide.

We rode the twenty miles or so out to the lake in a silence that was as comfortable as a long-let-out breath. The day, one of those damp, cold, still fall days, encouraged silence, so self-contained a flutter of movement would have been superfluous, and after we left the outskirts of town, there was none. The empty road wound up and down between the bare brown fields. The cornfields lay chopped and dormant, the cowless pastures were scruffy, tan stubble. Ahead of me my mother's flat red hat with its straight gray feather, serenely rode her nest of S-shaped curls. Next to me Stephen sat in his rich dark suit as if in a chitinous silence. Mr. Schaeffer talked now and then, but what he said did not, thanks be, much matter. On the cold plastic of the seat Stephen and I sat very distinct and separate. I would have liked to touch him, out of some sense of rebellion against my mother's guarding presence, but he seemed drugged, staring out of the window. When we passed Johnny's, I pressed his knee. He looked at me questioningly, and I shook my head. We were nearing the lake now, approaching the high palisade that guarded the Lake View Drive-

Inn. On summer nights its huge marquee spelled out the attractions with a buzzing blue-white heat. Now a dreary bunting covered it, stating in faded letters that it would open the night of April 1. And beside the Drive-Inn, as if clinging to its skirts, an orange-colored concrete hot-dog stand, a pink pizza palace, and a white Frostee Queen bar, all boarded over, left derelict, wrecked by the waning of the Drive-Inn, that dark-mouthed, glitter-eyed nymph that was, for the moment, out of season. Even so, passing this place, I had a brief, acute sense of a summer night there with Stephen, the warmth, the stale-sweet rankness of the car, the spluttering little sound box near our ears, the windshield congested with images that make a flickering colorful shade for our love. Something, a pulse, beat in my stomach. Inside my white angora gloves, my palms began to sweat.

After the drive-inn, there was only a mile or so to go. We made the turn from macadam to hardened mud and from mud to two rocky ruts that bounded behind the lake's cottage area. I preened for my first view of the water. In summer the view came in a sudden blue heart framed by two close-growing birches. Now the water appeared all at once but in less definite form, a diffuse horizontal streak of silver, gliding in and out between the birch trees' whiter branches. Schaeffer's cottage was at the top of the bluff and I winced as we galloped toward it, the Buick repeatedly scraping its belly on frozen grass hummocks. He pulled the car up behind his cottage, let the motor die, and said with a kind of proudful humility, "Well, folks, for what it is, this is it."

We got out stiffly but with smiles tuned to compliment, and followed Schaeffer around to the front. On the way, some fifteen yards, he thumped his fist against a clapboard, kicked the cement foundation at its corner, and booted a cigarette wrapper off the overgrown path. While he jingled his keys at the front door, we observed the view. We were on a little bluff that scurried abruptly down into the lake, or seemed to. No, I saw leaning over that there was a beach of sorts, or at least a stony take-off point. We looked out over the water. It was gray. Everything was gray, the grass on the bluff was yellow-gray, the stones and sandy patches dirty gray, the water a faint metallic gray-blue. The air was dense and the heavy sky seemed full of a hardening snow ready to drop. We couldn't see the opposite shore, an area of mist obscured it.

"Oh, it's lovely," my mother breathed. I shivered.

"It's pretty, all right," Schaeffer said. While we were contemplating, he had unlatched the shutters and pinned them back against the house. Now, as the door sprung open, a cold smell of kerosene leaked thinly out of the cottage. He darted in, we followed. The main room was, despite the opened shutters, still dark, the furniture was bulky and brown. There was a wide barrel-armed sofa, and a matching chair with a square hefty-woman spread of lap. There was a rocker, a table, and a tasseled lamp with a round china base, and a wall calendar which showed us a cute basketful of pink-ribboned kittens over the thick-black-numbered days of July, 1948. The room smelled of closed-up pine and kerosene.

"There's the kitchen," Schaeffer said, and looking over his shoulder we saw a black monster stove and a corner cupboard, cups hanging from hooks, each cup different.

"Upstairs," Schaeffer said, "we got two bedrooms and I put in a bath four-five years ago when Alice got too sick to go down to the water. I guess it doesn't seem like much, but then, we were always out a lot in the summer."

My mother was standing by the window looking out. "If you've got an indoor bath," she said, "what's that building?"

He peered over her shoulder. "It's kind of a garage-boathouse."

"Oh! Really? It's been years since I've been out in a boat. Not since my lost youth."

"Why, you're only a chicken," Schaeffer said heartily.

"An old hen is what you mean," my mother said, but gaily. She rustled the yellowed paper curtain at the window, and smiled. Smiling so she did look younger, the smile showed her deep one-sided dimple and her young white wide-spaced teeth. But this girlishness annoyed me. It made me feel old and stiff, like her mother.

"I don't suppose," she said, "that we could all take a turn around the lake? I suppose it would be too cold?"

"Good Lord, Mother," I said, "it's the middle of winter and Thanksgiving Day and we're all dressed up."

"Why," Schaeffer said easily, "there shouldn't be any danger. Long as nobody rocks the boat we'll all stay high and dry. She's a pretty safe tub, anyway. No motor but good oars."

"I'm not setting foot in any boat," I said. "You're always complaining about how much I spend on clothes and I just bought these shoes last week and now you want me to ru-in them."

"Take them off," my mother suggested calmly.

"And freeze?" I asked.

"—uh—" Stephen said, "maybe Ellie and I could just walk around."

"These children," my mother said to Schaeffer, "they have absolutely no gumption. Is it really too cold to go out?"

"Heck no," Schaeffer said. He had already slipped off his suit jacket and from a hook on the back of the kitchen door had lifted a large khaki sweater. "Might need a little help, young fella," he said to Stephen. Reluctantly, I could see, Stephen took off his jacket and rolled up his white shirt sleeves and followed Schaeffer out the front door to the boat shed. My mother and I went out to watch.

"Honestly," I said, feeling grim.

"Hmm?" she said.

"Mr. Schaeffer certainly did not want to go for a boat ride in his best suit in the middle of winter."

"I don't see any ice out there."

"Suppose you tip over?"

"Darling, I've been getting along all these years on land as on the sea. I wish you'd take better care of yourself instead of worrying about your poor old mother."

"Funny," I said, "in reverse, that's exactly the way I feel."

She turned her face away to observe the men's progress. Schaeffer and Stephen staggered out of the boat shed, the aluminum tub dropping from their hands like a stiff silver corpse. They came to the edge of the bluff; here the struggle began. They had to get the boat down into the water without damaging its fine slick skin. They went over, Schaeffer first, shouting "Hold it! Hold it!" while the prow of the boat tipped up. The prow bit into the air, then dipped as the stern rose, and Stephen turned sideways, leaning, bending lower and lower until finally he dropped off the edge of the bluff after the boat and was gone. In a moment they reappeared on the stony beach below, stumbling between rocks with their cold goose freight.

"Hold it! Hold it!" Schaeffer yelled again and slowly they lowered the boat into the water. Then Schaeffer bent, rolled up his pant legs, took off his shoes and socks and laid them aside. At the water's edge he took a new grip on the boat and plunged in. I winced.

"Hey," he shouted, now in cold water up to his twiglike calves, "not bad, ladies. Come on in."

My mother began making preparations for her descent. She took off her gloves and snapped them inside her purse, then, grasping my arm, removed her shoes. Carrying her shoes in her right hand and her purse in her left, she too walked to the bluff and disappeared down it in stages: first her legs, then her straight gray coat, last the red hat and the staunch little feather. She too reappeared on the cobbly beach, walking sedately, the way fakirs do toward fire. As she reached the boat, Schaeffer grabbed her arm to help her in.

"Allee-oop," he said, shoving. She clambered aboard; the boat rocked violently until Schaeffer tamed it, and it came to a bobbing obedient wobble under his hand. My mother laughed, a distant string of chimes, and climbed carefully to the stern, still holding her shoes. Schaeffer shoved off and hopped in, then took the center seat and fitted the oars to the gunwales. From the stern my mother waved gravely, like a child on a merry-go-round. Schaeffer began to row, turning the boat prow-out. Stephen clambered over the bluff and stood next to me and we both watched until my mother's hat bobbed past the curve of the shore. Strange, though, I could still clearly hear the plop of Schaeffer's oars.

"Did you get your suit wet?" I asked, turning at last to him. He looked blue with cold.

"Nah," he said, and bending, spilled sand out of his cuffs. Standing, he looked at me and smiled. Without talk, we took hands and went back to Schaeffer's cottage.

"God it's cold!" he said. He closed the cottage door. He rolled down his sleeves and put on his jacket and began searching his pockets for cigarettes. I sat down on the brown sofa, huddling into a corner for warmth. It seemed colder inside than out. My breath projected from me in a long cloud and the lit cigarette Stephen handed to me was a small cheery inferno. He dropped down beside me and we smoked. Gradually, my tiny furnace diminished, and at the exact moment it should have been scorching my glove, Stephen pinched it out of my fingers and stood up. He went to the door and tossed both butts out.

"Have a nice swim," he said to them and came back, with a tense grin, to me. He sat down and the sofa springs twanged. The pulse that I had felt passing the Drive-Inn began again.

"Long time no see," he said, facing me and putting an arm on the back of the sofa.

"Wednesday," I said, looking at my lap instead of him. "That's not so long."

"That was math class. School doesn't count, does it?"

"Ha."

"You know what I think? You're a grind, a little girl-grind."

I looked up at him angrily, and then saw he was smiling. It was his smile I think, that made me love him, so rare after all his coldness. It unfolded crookedly along his face, deepening the declivities, and I traced the line next to his mouth in awe. He caught my gloved hand, then with his other hand touched the back of my neck, making me shiver.

"We're not meant for each other," I said, "we're both so cold."

"It's only temporary," he said and laid his face against mine. And then put his cold lips on mine, and then after we had kissed our faces warm, unbuttoned my coat and cupped his hand, gently, around my breast.

. . . . .

We kissed for a long time. It was as if we were on a long, delightful journey, the destination not quite known: first, paddling along on a brown, sun-spattered river, the banks grassy, the trees tame, slipping gradually into a lush, green gloom, the bent trees thick, vine hung, the banks overgrown with climbing things. Above us the warning caw of hidden birds. All through the last kisses, which were a long dark vortex, I kept thinking I heard my mother's silvery laugh. I sat up, Stephen groaned.

"Jesus," he said, "what's wrong?"

"Nothing," I said. "Would you like a cigarette?"

He looked odd, his hair mussed, the lids of his eyes puffy.

"No," he said in a tight voice and closed his eyes and put his head back on the sofa. "Sometimes I wish you were Nora Novak."

"Thank you," I said. He put his hand on my back between my shoulder blades, exactly over the place where my bra hooked.

"Hey," he said. "How old are you?"

"Eighty."

"No, really."

"Fifteen."

"That young?"

"I'll be sixteen in May."

"You know something, you're just a kid. It's a good thing you have me to watch out for you. How come you're so young? Did you skip?"

"I'm intelligent, that's how come. How come you're so old, did you stay back?"

"I was sick a lot one year, in the second grade. Hey, did I tell you I heard from my brother?"

"No, where is he? Korea?"

"Yeah. He sent me some money. He said he'd send me some every month and I could save it for college. Only, I bought this suit."

"Oh, Stephen," I said and looked at him.

"I didn't have a good suit. Except a blue one I graduated from junior high in and that one was my father's."

"All right," I said.

"We can't all be rich."

"I *know*. Why is it you think I'm so rich? My mother's good coat is eight years old and we're practically taking in boarders."

"Listen, if you wanted to go to college they'd say, 'Step right up, Miss Munson, we love to have your type of girl,' but they're going to take one look at me and lock up the till."

"Who tells you such things, Stephen? Where do you get your crazy ideas?"

And, as if laughing in answer, I heard my mother's voice climbing the bluff. We moved apart; he lit a cigarette. She came in a moment later with Schaeffer behind her. She was red-cheeked and her hat sat too far back on her head and she was still carrying her shoes.

"Hello," she caroled. "Have a nice walk? We had such a lovely ride."

"Got kind of cold, though," Schaeffer said and slammed the door. He had put on his shoes but not his socks, and the rolled-up pants legs flapped above his knobby ankles.

"I'm glad you got back," I said. "Safe and sound."

"Indeed we are," my mother said. She sat down on the fat armchair and put on her shoes. "Do you know what I think we need, Ed? Some coffee. Do you have any?"

Schaeffer, with grunts and angular bends, like a derrick descending on a brick, had taken off his shoes, and was brushing the sand off his feet.

"Nope, I don't think we do have any coffee, Frieda, but I bet I've got a little something else somewhere. I always do keep some whisky for emergencies."

"Oh," my mother said, "I'm not much of a drinker."

"One drink won't hurt. And you don't want to let yourself get cold, Frieda."

"Well, you'll have to tell me what to do, Ed, I've never made a drink in my life."

"Sit still, sit right there." Schaeffer got up, stamping into his shoes. "Don't you move a muscle. I'll fix the fixings, long as the pipes aren't clogged." He went out into the kitchen and we heard a squawk. "Nope," he yelled, "pipes all right."

"If you're going to give the children drinks, Ed, you'd better make my daughter's weak. She's never had one before."

Stephen grinned, I glared, my mother crossed her legs and rubbed at a spot of mud on her shoe. "Now, just look at that," she said, extending her foot and moving it up and down, "I've had these shoes four years and you'd never know it."

Schaeffer came out of the kitchen holding all our tumblers between his hands and my mother, taking her glass, proposed a toast. "To more and better boat rides," she said.

"Hear, hear," said Schaeffer. My mother and Schaeffer had another drink and then we all drove home.

The ride home was wild. My mother and Schaeffer sang duets. He sang in a dull monotone, and her clear voice carried the tune. They sang "A Pretty Girl" and "You Were Meant for Me" and "There's a Small Hotel."

"They don't write 'em like that anymore," Schaeffer said. In the dark behind their voices, Stephen and I held hands.

"You've got a fine voice," Schaeffer was saying to my mother. "You must have a good musical ear."

"I used to love music but I don't listen much anymore. When I was a girl I thought I wanted to study music, but then there were so many things I wanted to do. And my father was very old-fashioned. He thought women should be educated only enough to make them genteel. So he let me take piano lessons."

"Is that right? There now, I knew you were a talented woman."

"Oh, but I haven't played in years. And now my hands are much too stiff. Sully, that's my daughter who lives in California, has a wonderful sense of rhythm. She was such a good dancer. And when Eleanor was just a tiny thing she wrote the most wonderful poems, so she must have a good ear too. Eleanor, how did that poem go, the one you wrote for the SPCA contest?"

"Good Lord, I don't know, Mother, I was only six or seven."

"Something about the doe and its foe . . ."

" 'How doth the busy little doe . . .' "

"Oh, don't be silly. It was a very nice poem and won first prize in the contest."

"It must be a real satisfaction," Schaeffer said, "to have such a talented family. Is Dr. Munson musical too?"

"Why, yes, once he was. And Louis, my son, could play almost anything by ear."

As we came into Clifton and headed downtown, my mother said less and less until, when we arrived, we were as silent as we'd begun. Stephen got into his car and drove away and Schaeffer drove off. My mother and I went upstairs. My father was out. "Gone to movies," his note said, "Sully called, says Happy Thanksgiving, no other news."

My mother picked at her coat buttons and took off her hat. I went into the bedroom to get undressed and she came in after I was in bed. She pulled off her clothes listlessly and left them lying on a heap on her small blue chair. This was something she never did and I could see that she was upset after all, at having missed talking to Sully.

8

"You did what?" my father said and looked at me over a corner of the *Clifton Advocate Times*. At four-thirty on the Monday after Thanksgiving it was almost dark and my father was sitting in the red living-room chair nearest the front windows, hunched to get the last of the rosy light. I had told him as soon as I'd taken my coat off, partly to get it done, partly because I knew he'd take it less hard than my mother.

"Failed the math," I said again and he took the report card I held out to him. I sat down on the other side of the coffee table and picked up a magazine that had come in the morning's mail.

"Hmm," he said, orienting himself, "let's see. 'English—90, Chemistry—80, Latin—90, Social Studies—80.' Is that good? I thought you liked history."

"The teacher is stupid," I said and folded the magazine to an article called "Teen-Age Syphilis: Not even their mothers know," and my father said:

"Possible, but not likely. Now, this is an interesting mark, this—er—53."

"Isn't it interesting," I agreed. "The trouble is, I have to get 75 on the final to pass."

He put the card down on the table and looked at me tentatively. He cleared his throat. "I suppose," he began, "that this report is not really very bad."

I laughed.

He looked at me perplexed. "Why are you laughing?"

"It's the worst report card I've ever gotten."

"Is there something humorous about that?" He picked up his newspaper and began refolding it, a complex, noisy process. "I hope your mother will find this equally funny."

I sighed and looked down at the magazine. The photograph accompanying the article was of a teen-age girl, back turned to camera, head bent in despair. There. Now I'd done it. I had counted on his vagueness, a kind of mental buffer which often shielded me from my mother's perceptions. Now my laughter had undermined the careful groundwork I'd laid. Why had I laughed? Because it was all working out so well.

Downstairs, the heavy glass of the outer door rattled in the wrought-iron frame, the inner door opened and closed. The switch snapped and a wedge of yellow light glided into the living room, darkening it.

"Hello?" my mother called coming up the stairs, and then from the doorway said, "You two! Sitting in the dark. Heaven help us, we're not that poor." She tossed her packages into the chair nearest the door and pulled the string of the standing lamp. Under its light she looked ruddy and young. "What a melancholy group, and I feel so *good*. You'll never guess what your old mother did today, Eleanor, my dear." She pulled off her frazzled, black wool gloves and tossed them as elegantly as if they were kid onto the stack of packages, and then lifted her arms to unpin her hat. It was her everyday hat, a squashed drum of brown velour to which clung a limp hunk of veiling. "I bought a dress," she said, smiling. "For myself. A red one. I told the salesgirl I was too old for red and she laughed. I thought she laughed sincerely so I tried it on."

My father adjusted the paper with a snap. "Have you ever known a sincere sales person?" he asked.

"It fit beautifully, and I thought, why not."

My father looked stern. "Frieda," he said, "your daughter has some distressing news."

My mother stopped smiling and came to where I was sitting. She looked down into my face, lifted her hand as if to touch my forehead, but instead dropped it bashfully into her coat pocket. "You're not sick?" she asked.

I picked up the report card from the table and gave it to her. She shook her head. "I don't have my reading glasses." I read out the marks in a slow, bored voice. She stood listening with her head tilted and her hands in her pockets. My father pretended to read the paper.

"That's it," I said when I'd finished and put the card face down on the table. "Really, you don't have to look like death. It's not the first time anyone's failed."

"That's right," my father said, grinning and lowering temporarily his newsprint screen. "Didn't I read somewhere last week that as a boy Winston Churchill failed mathematics? In that case, ha ha ha, Eleanor is certainly on the right road."

My mother turned and went into the kitchen. I heard the

refrigerator door open and close and I went out and stood in the doorway. She had gotten milk and eggs out of the refrigerator and her coat was still on. I waited for her to say something, but she worked instead on the stapled-down cover of the egg box.

"I've got to go out tonight," I said.

She turned and reached up into the cupboard to get a bowl, then did what I had feared all these minutes she would do, looked at me. The bowl was clutched in her hands, her eyes were small and bright. She laughed.

I went out to the living room and put on my coat. "See you later," I said to my father.

"Ha!" he said. He had finally put on the lamp and was now deep in the editorial, with which he nightly, lovingly battled. I ran down the stairs and out of the door. At the corner I found I'd forgotten my wallet, scarf, and gloves, but I couldn't go back, and so I began walking up the long hill toward Stephen's.

Downtown this time of night was a purple kingdom full of pushing crowds. The Clifton peasants were leaving their looms. From Houghton's, buses packed black with people arrived and deposited their crushed loads at the stop in front of City Drug. Girls, dyers and weavers, typists, file clerks, pushed along Hill Street in twos and threes, getting a quick cigarette before the next bus came. Their faces looked empty, innocent, jaded, wise, lost. The block's two bars, Danny's Swan Room and the Kom-on-out Klub, were going full tilt, signs flashing, doors swinging, music alternately blasting and fading, men and girls going in and out. The streets seemed full of danger. Horns blared, whistles shrilled, headlights bent and swerved, and I walked quickly. It was damp and cold. The lights of the mill as I finally approached it seemed false, the treacherous lights of a swamp. Stephen's house was dark and I went down the steep steps feeling scared. Suppose that other Wojcik, his father, should open the door? I kept the outer door open as I groped for the iron handle of the old-fashioned doorbell. I turned it; it made a rusty clang, more of a scrape than a ring. Beyond the dark door I could hear, like an imperfect third door, a lattice of television noise. The hall light went on, lighting the colored glass squares. The door opened a crack and Rosemary peered out.

She was in a pink corduroy bathrobe so loosely tied that a fat triangle of blue nightgown showed in the top. "Gee," she said, her eyes widening, "I thought you were Steve," and either from cold or surprise she clenched the top of the robe together.

Oh, I said, isn't he home? He wasn't in school, I thought he was sick.

"Nah," she said, "he's never sick, he had to go somewhere for his father."

Oh, I said, well, could I stay and wait?

"Sure, okay," she said and opened the door all the way. Then, turning, pulled herself up and tightened the belt of her robe. Startlingly, as she did so, a loose seam over her hip gave way, a welt which, slowly opening, looked at me in nightgown blue. I followed her through the hall. Today the yellowish smell of cauliflower obscured something darkly pleasant that I couldn't at once identify. In the living room the TV salesman held up a box of soap, and as we passed Rosemary snapped him off so brutally that he died with his mouth ajar.

"I keep the noise on all day," she said, "even though I don't really listen. For company, see? I like a little noise in the house. I grew up in a big family, my old lady had twelve kids, can you beat that? Yeah, I grew up with a crowd, let me tell you."

In the kitchen I saw with surprise that she was baking. The room was warm, the smell of chocolate now vivid. On the table stood assorted pieces of used cooking equipment, a ransacked box of cake mix, a beer can with a smoking cigarette laid perilously on its rim, and next to this a cracked white plate stacked with chocolate cupcakes.

"Take off your coat, have a Coke. No, we ain't got Coke, want a beer? When I cook I taste so much I get thirsty." She got me a can of beer from the refrigerator, opened it, and thrust it at me, then asked herself, "Now, where the hell was I?" She stood, hands on hips, looking around the kitchen. "I don't cook much, but when I do I get so rattled it hardly ever comes out right. And with a mix yet. I swear to God, I got short-changed on sense." She took a burnt-edged dish towel from the stove, investigated the innards of the oven, and satisfied, let the door slam and the dish towel drop. She seemed different today than the first time I'd seen her, despite the flat gold bedroom sandals, taller and sturdier. Her figure, in the long pink robe, was tall and full. She wore no makeup and without it her face looked less mouthy, her eyes larger—almost too large and brown, and the blanched freckles that dusted her nose were the color of cinnamon. Two lines that ran from the flanges of her nose to her mouth gave her face a certain thoughtful force. Today she seemed solid and classically graceful, and I could not believe what I'd heard about her.

"Every once in a while," she said, dropping down in the chair across from me, "I get goo-hungry. I just gotta have a bite of something sweet so I make myself something. Today I didn't feel so hot, an' I stayed in bed all morning, an' then, you figure, it gets past two, what's the sense of getting dressed. Here, have a cupcake." She pushed the plate toward me. I said, no thanks, that I'd just finish the beer. She took a cupcake and carefully shook it free of crumbs, then ate it.

" 'S a funny thing, different people get hungry for different things. Now, me, like I say, I every once in a while got to have something sweet. Pete, that's Steve's brother, he used to have a steak a week. Had to have it, yeah, that's a fact. We'd come in late a Saturday night, Mickey and me, and the kid woulda lifted the steak for Sunday out of the icebox and he'd be standing by the stove frying it. Mike used to give 'im hell"—she sucked in her breath and it came out loud, like her husband's—"STEALIN', the kid's STEALIN' my food, right from under my NOSE." Then her voice condensed sedately. "My husband, Mike, is kind of like that too. He's got to have his beer." She smiled at me.

"Now, I can't figure out what Steve is. I guess he's kind of a goo-eater, like me." She picked up another cupcake. "So you thought he was sick?"

I said I didn't know, but he was always in school and today was the day we got report cards.

"Hey," she said, "that's why he was so mad. Any other kid'd jump at the chance to take a day offa school. Not him, though, no sir. Me, I never liked school much. I did okay but I was never too good. I took typing and shorthand and all that stuff, then I end up at the mill. Seven to four shift in the loom room. Like all the other girls. And we all thought we was going to be secretaries. Ha. You taking typing?"

I shook my head. No, I said, I was planning to go to college. If I passed math. I made it sound dubious, my passing math, for here, in this kitchen, it didn't seem at all bad to be failing, and indeed, Rosemary smiled at me and winked.

"What the hell, who needs it? I mean, so you don't add, some guy'll do it for you. Stevie's good at that crap, let him do it."

I laughed and she gave me a peculiar look, then licked her fingers and in a brisk, business like way rubbed chocolate crumbs from her hands. She leaned toward me, folding her arms on the table, and as I looked her large breasts were pushed together and up in the nest of her arms. The nightgown's lace gaped so far forward I could see the rusty rims of her nipples. I looked away, up at the wall. The wall calendar, Our Lady of something in red and blue, stared back at me in anguish. I wondered how often Stephen saw

Rosie dressed this way. When I looked at her face again, she was still scrutinizing mine.

"You know what," she said, "you look like a nice kid and maybe I don't have to tell you this, and maybe I do. I can't figure out how wise you are. I mean, when I was fifteen-sixteen I was pretty darn wise, but then, I always kind of knew what the score was." She paused and looked at me. I expected her to go ahead and warn me about what I was getting into but she said, "You know something? Everybody's got a sweet side, even Mike's sweet sometimes, but some people got more than others. What I mean is, Stevie's an awful sweet kid, and he don't know A from B yet. Do you read me?"

I nodded, as if I did.

"See," she said, "now he's getting all hooked on this college stuff. He's got about as much chance of it as I got to kiss the Pope's toe, and he might as well forget it. His father ain't putting out no dough for him to go and waste his time, and if you been sticking these bugs in his ear, you better quit."

I found I was clutching the beer can in both hands. But, goodness, I said, Stephen was very smart and he could get a scholarship. They gave scholarships to smart boys. She laughed a coarse, short laugh, and picked up her pack of cigarettes. With the long bright nails of her thumb and forefinger she pried a cigarette out of the pack.

"Listen to her! You gonna arrange it? Don't you think I know who gets the scholarships? They don't give 'em to poor Polacks. You pay for everything you get in life, I know that. Anyway, what's he want to go to college for? So he reads a couple of books, he can read books here. What's he going to get out of it, huh?"

I said, uh, I thought he would make more money.

"Yeah?" she said. "If he listened to his father he could make his pile. More, anyway, than most people in this town. He's got a wood head, though, you know? Stubborn. Wants to do things his way." She lit her cigarette with a masculine wave and dropped the burnt match into the empty beer can. It sizzled and she looked at me suspiciously. "What are you going to be? A teacher?"

No, I said, I did not want to be a teacher.

She looked severe, like someone handing out a questionnaire. "Then what do you want to go for?"

I looked down at the beer can, but my own face gleaming metallically back at me was no help. Drawn to a polished length, owl-eyed, suddenly long chinned, it looked teacherish. It was like the ironic assertion of a truth I kept avoiding. And I had gone to such anxious lengths to conceal my pedantry. I had crushed my vocabulary into jazzy monosyllabic grunts; I had given up raising my hand in class. What I wanted her to see was the Technicolor vision I had of myself, Queen of Sigma something, sitting legs crossed on a large beer keg while below me handsome letter-men drained their steins and toasted me in song. But I couldn't, because of Stephen, bring up these things. My silence made her confident.

"Yeah," she said, "I guess it's nice to learn all about painters and books and stuff like that. I don't know, I never liked to read much. But you know what I think? These ladies, the educated ones like that Mrs. Littrell, the dentist's wife, and Mrs. Simpson, and that crowd, I don't think they're any better than me, from what I hear around town, the way they carry on at that club, and if they're no better than me, what's the point?"

I knew that Mrs. Littrell, the chairwoman of the Book Meetings, had been for a while to a girls' college outside of Boston, and I knew that Mrs. Simpson had gone to some place in Pennsylvania, but I had never thought of them as educated. They were simply those citizen-wives who ran the Girl Scout committees and the Concert Association and the Women's Club. I had supposed that this was one of the uses of attending college, like needing a license to drive. After all, someone had to run these things. Once, though, I had heard my mother say to my father that Mrs. Littrell was "so stupid it makes me want to scream" and I myself knew Mrs. Simpson was. I didn't know how to explain this to Rosemary. The best I could manage was to say I didn't know.

She laughed. Her left hand came flat down on the table and her rings cracked against the wood. "Hey," she said, "that's a hot one. I don't either. I'm twenty-six years old, and I don't know a goddam thing except where I'm going to sleep tonight and who with. Sometimes I think that's not a hell of a lot to know."

She got up slowly, pushing herself up from the table with both hands. She accumulated the cooking stuff in the mixing bowl and carried this to the sink. There she opened the cupboard door and looked at herself in a small mirror that was taped to the inside of the door. "Christ," she said anxiously, "I look God-awful. These crummy days I stay in bed. I don't know, I get these days I just want to sleep and sleep. I can't think of much else to do. I get tired of walking around downtown. I got four sisters and I never see 'em they got so many kids. I don't know what it is with Mike and me, we just aren't lucky that way. I been to that Doctor Kendricks, you know? The one who feels around in your insides? And I had all these tests and, I don't know, I'm supposed to be in such swell shape but nothing happens." She laughed. "It's not like we don't try." She ran water over the dishes in the sink and pushed her hair back out of her face with her wrist. The robe, I saw, had fallen slack again; the eye-shaped welt had healed. I took a long swallow of the beer and for the first time in the year I'd been drinking it, liked its taste—it tasted bitter but buoyant and strong, a taste of what I wanted out of life.

That minute I heard someone come clattering down the steps and slam through the doors and from the hall Stephen yelled, "Hey, Rosie," and then came and stood in the doorway to the kicthen, looking at me.

Whenever we met and it was unexpected he had a technique of looking at me coldly. His face would go rigid and long while I never failed to smile, hating myself for it. 'Oh," he said, "hi."

"There's thanks," I said. "I walk all this way to see if you're sick and you look like, drop dead."

"I'm surprised, that's all."

From the sink Rosemary unexpectedly took my side. "He's always dead-pan," she said to me, and then to him, "He say he'd be home?"

"Yeah, about ten," Stephen said, coming all the way into the kitchen. He picked up a cupcake. "I had to go somewhere for my father. Christ, the bastard wouldn't even let me catch a lunch."

"Oh, cut it out, Steve, huh?" Rosemary said. He looked at her, swallowed the cupcake almost whole, and took another. "So how'd you do?" he asked.

"Do how?" I asked, although I knew he meant the math. "Oh, that. All right."

"Yeah? Come on, I'll give you a ride home." I stood up and pulled on my coat and he took two more cupcakes—"For pete's sake," Rosemary yelled and threw the burnt towel after us. We laughed and went out to the car.

"So what did you get?" he asked, as I got in.

"Ninety-nine," I said.

"Come on."

"Ninety-eight."

He laughed.

"Don't you want to know what you got?"

"I know. Ninety-five or ninety-seven because that jerk always takes off three points for neatness."

"One hundred," I said, and in the dark of the car leaned toward him and squeezed his arm. "You're so smart."

"How about that?" he marveled. "I am, aren't I?"

"A genius," I said. He put his arm around me and peered up at the car roof. "Let's see, that gives me—uh—

should be—uh—Je-sus—hot dog—ninety-seven for the term. How's that, huh? Pretty good, huh!" In his glee, he squeezed my shoulder hard. Up until that moment I had been honestly happy for him, now I felt stiff and tired.

"I don't know why you care," I said, looking out of the side window. "If you're not going to college."

"Who told you that? Rosemary?"

"She thinks I've been sticking bugs in your ears."

"They don't want me to go."

"Do you want to?"

"Yeah, I guess so, I don't know, I don't know what to do about it. I mean, I don't know what kind of place would take a slob like me. I'm so stupid I can hardly spell my own name."

That made me smile. "It's a hard name," I said. "You ought to go, Stephen, you know you ought to." He was half turned toward me in the car, one hand on the back of the seat, the other on the steering wheel.

"If my brother keeps sending me money, I might make it. He's been a good guy. I figure if he sends me money this year and next I can get through a year someplace and if I do okay—"

"You'll do fine," I said, and then began to cry.

"Hey," he said, "hey, what's with you? You passed, didn't you?"

I shook my head and tears slipped coldly off my chin.

"Hey," he said, "don't cry. Listen, I'm going to help you, no kidding. What do you care if you fail, anyway, huh? You're the prettiest girl in the class. You want to be smart and look like Agnes Pearson?" He tightened his arm around me and said close to my ear, "Ellie, El, don't cry. Listen, I've been wanting to tell you, I don't know why I want to, except I can't help it, and I'm not much good at saying anything, but like today, I didn't see you all day and I missed you so, I felt so empty inside and scared, it's as if there's nothing else I want to do but see you and be with you. Ellie? I guess"—he laughed and a funny fault grew in his voice—"I love you, that's all I can figure out."

I leaned against him, crying, then slowly the tears stopped and I rubbed my cheek dry on the shoulder of his jacket. He held me. I began to feel immensely warm, sleepy, and relaxed, as if a slow push of lava were feeding my veins. I thought of going home and didn't want to. Home was miles away, across a cold desert of purple sand. My home was a high boat, looming up over the desert, and my parents two ghosts whom I feared and feared for, condemned to sail forever in their silent moored ship, wandering from spar to spar. And the desert sand so cold, the moon up there a fingernail snippet of steel, the stars screwed tight into the sky, and next to Stephen I was warm. I wanted to stay in the dark, humid car, next to his brown, chocolate breath. I lifted my face to the wool-warmed side of his neck and said, "I don't want to go home yet," and he said, kissing me, no, not yet, and for a long while I stayed there, in the bower of his arms, warmed, nourished, fed, protected by the knowledge of his love.

9

What I had always feared about my mother's anger was the way it went underground. The whole of that week she was silent and I avoided her silence. I left for school earlier in the morning, and stayed late to work in the school library. On Tuesday I went up to Patty's, on Wednesday Stephen and I worked together in the public library. On Thursday I went to a missionary's lecture at church, but on Friday there was nowhere to go. Patty was sick, Stephen was working, the library closed at six, and everyone I called was out. There was nothing to do but stay at home.

It began like all the other evenings I had ever spent there: quietly. Our house always gave me a high sense of separateness. The other buildings, the Pickwick Building, the Elks' Club, the Mohawkin Mill, stood packed together closely, but our driveways separated us from the others as if we were a small stone island. And at the Y, at the Elks' Club, the changing pattern of lights, the odd range of noises, from dormant to dance band, made them seem perfectly transient, like pleasure boats that passed us in the night. Our noise was negligible but steady, and now, with the storm windows attached, and the Venetian blinds dropped, and the drapes pulled across, we sat as if sealed inside so many boxes. Outside, like another curtain, a stiff and lacy layer of snow was falling.

After the dinner dishes were done, my mother and I, walking yards apart, went to the living room. From the bedroom she brought her sewing in a large tapestry bag and sat down with it, in a corner of the sofa. She was embroidering a tablecloth for Sully, a long piece of yellow linen, the tulips on it square-cornered, stamped in faint blue crosses. I think she knew Sully would never use it—my own idea of Sully was swiping a damp dishrag across a plastic place mat—but my mother had always embroidered for Christmas. Sitting in the pallid puddle of light made by the underfed standing lamp, she was quiet. There was no sound except the breathless whisk of the thread going through the cloth. She did not look up. To embroider or do any close work, she had lately acquired glasses, and her face, foreshortened from my view, was comfortably hidden by the curve of her pink bone frames.

I got my books from the dumping chair next to the door and surveyed the field. Tonight the only homework left to do was Latin. Since Miss Macready in her methodical way had checked on A through L today, I knew that on Monday I would be asked to translate. I took up the Latin grammar, a frayed orange and green, and carefully sat down in the armless red-plush chair. I chose this place neither for comfort nor lighting but because it was at an angle from my mother: if she looked directly up she would see not me but the dining room, and at the end of the hall, the kitchen. I opened my book to the assignment and read the Latin words over first because, without any applied intellect, they sounded so fine. In the kitchen I heard my father going through his medicines as he did every night after dinner, and the clink of these bottles was vaguely disturbing. I was at this moment happy in silence and I knew that presently my father would come in and destroy the delicate amusical balance that stretched on such taut strings between my mother and myself. And he did. He came slowly from the direction of the kitchen into the living room with a hand on his vest, and his after-dinner expression of resigned pain. Passing me, he belched loudly, then sat in the chair opposite me and next to my mother.

"Winter," he announced, "is here." From the round coffee table, littered with the day's accumulation of literature and mail, he took a large book, its color the rusty brown of all corroded hope, and opened it on his knees and muttered as he turned the pages, "If anyone cares."

My mother's lips pursed, her thread whisked briskly. "I care, I certainly do care. In fact, all I think about is next month and the oil bill." She snipped a thread, shook out the cloth and examined it, then bunched a blank tulip in her hand for forcing. "I hope the new apartment will be warm enough. It should be, after all it cost to create."

"Mmm," my father said, tracing down a line of print with his finger. He slammed the book shut, then opened it again in the middle, the way we were taught in Sunday School to find the Book of Psalms. "Ahh," he said.

"You might show a little interest," my mother said.

"It's your project, Frieda," my father said. He looked up at the standing lamp, which hunched balefully between my mother and himself, and gave off, under its cracked parchment shade, such an imbecile glow. "Someday," he said, "we should have night-long light from the sun. And heat. Solar energy for year-round use. The sidewalks will trap it. We'll never have to shovel another foot of snow. All the downtown stores will have reflecting panels. It'll be as warm in Clifton as it is in—uh—St. Petersburg, Florida."

"I've never really liked warm weather," my mother said.

"Every home-owner will have his own reflecting and absorbing panels and there won't be any heat bills to worry about."

"Until that day," my mother said, "we pay. Is anyone else warm?" She did not look at either of us as she said this and indeed, the question was largely rhetorical. It came every evening at this same time. In October my father began wearing a cardigan sandwiched between his coat and vest and he was always, grudgingly, "all right." My mother, who never wore a sweater except when she worked outside in the fall, was without fail, warm. I had inherited my father's eccentric circulation but was too vain to pad myself like a coolie. Now my mother got up, marched over my father's feet to the thermostat, read it with a grave, surprised look, pushed it down, and returned, stepping over my feet as if they were rocks in her path.

"If anyone is cold," she said, "winter's the time for a sweater."

I already wore a sweater and so I simply went on reading

the Latin and wondering why the little words, *quis, quid,* like troublesome gnats, merely buzzed meaninglessly in my ears. My mother gathered her work on her lap.

"Schaeffer says the apartment will be ready to rent on the first. I'll put an ad in the *Times* on Saturday."

"Fine, fine, fine," my father said.

"I hope the apartment will fill a few financial gaps."

My father looked bored, slumped back in his chair, scratched his head, and propped the book upon his chest. "Money can do anything," he said.

"Almost," my mother said, cheerfully.

My father sat up straight, yawned, and stretched. "I don't know why it is, no one likes to visit the MD when it snows."

"Or rains," my mother said to her cloth, "or shines."

"I think it has something to do with the weight of ions. I understand that on rainy days the ions are heavier and therefore tend to have a depressing effect, quite literally, mind you—"

"I hope," my mother said, "that whoever does move in will be quiet."

My father squinted up at the ceiling. "You know what I think, Frieda, we ought to take the first month's rent and install acoustic ceilings. TV sets, wild parties, lovers' quarrels, right here in our own living room. Good God. Eleanor had better study this week, next may be too late."

I made a noise in my throat; my father looked across the room in feigned surprise. "Why there she is! What are you doing home tonight?"

"Her boyfriend," my mother said, "must be ill."

"Stephen is working," I said. "Daddy, what makes you think I go out every night?"

"Don't you?" he asked. His raised eyebrows made two clownish arcs of incredulity.

"No," I said.

"What restraint," my mother said.

I slammed my Latin book shut. "You will be delighted to know that he's going away over the holidays. He has a job in Albany."

"How industrious," my mother said.

"He certainly is," my father exclaimed. "I think that's fine, very commendable. He'll get ahead."

My mother snorted; I started, with some dignity, to reexamine the subjunctive mode.

"By the way," my father said, "how's your math?"

"What?" I asked.

"Your mathematics," my father repeated. "Is it improving?"

"In four days?" I said. "Really, Father, miracles went out with J. Christ."

My father, perturbed, looked at my mother, as if to ask how she could account for me. My mother drew the corners of her mouth in.

"Were she as smart as she likes to sound she'd be getting straight A's."

"I did pass a math quiz this morning," I said.

"Sixty-five?" my mother asked.

"Eight," I said.

"Grand," she said. "Run right to Radcliffe and ask for a scholarship."

I considered. "I don't think I want to go to Radcliffe."

"Who was it," my father pondered, "oh, yes, I know, Da Giami, the druggist, now, his daughter is going to some place—let me think—Hobart, Hubbard, Hibert? Ah, well, at any rate he seemed to think it a good school."

"It's Catholic," I said, although I didn't, in fact, know the place.

"Oh," he said.

"I don't suppose," my mother said, removing her glasses and addressing me directly, at last, "that you have had the time to inquire about tutoring?"

"I did ask, and Mr. Martin said he'd do it."

"Martin!" my father said. "Well, that's very nice. To take up his time that way."

"It's not free, Daddy," I said.

"It's not?" he said.

"Everything in life costs money," I said. "Two-fifty an hour is what he charges."

"Two-fifty an hour!"

"Oh, stop it, Fred," my mother said. "Did you ever stop to think how much you spend on gasoline, driving around to get those impossible books, and how much useless plate glass you've got stacked away with molds in it, to say nothing of the amount you yourself spend on medication. What's two-fifty an hour?"

"Frieda," my father said, "it's the principle. L-E not A-L. Education is a privilege, not a right. I just want your daughter to realize how much the process costs. Blood, toil, tears, sweat, and money."

"Oh, money," my mother said, and laughed. Then it was very quiet. The shelf clock struck once—it was eight-thirty—long past the time the waiting room should have been full of shuffling people. My father turned pages, scratched, shifted, mumbled, and, occasionally, laughed. My mother's threat dipped under the yellow cloth and came out carrying on its thin blue back a little darting sliver of light. The Latin did not march and my old trouble, intense sleepiness, was coming on. Suddenly, downstairs, the outer door slammed. My mother sat straight up; my father's eyebrows surged.

"Ah," he said, and turned a page.

"Fred," my mother said.

"Hmm?" he said.

"Someone came in downstairs," she said. He rose wearily, and as he did so, she leaned forward and picked a thread off his suit. He went down the stairs. In a little while he came back up.

"Wind," he said, and sat down again. The clock bonged nine. My mother got up, brushed past him and went clicking down the stairs. I heard the lock being sprung and the testing rattle of the knob, then the click of the downstairs switch. She came back up the stairs and stood in the doorway, looking not at me but at my father.

"Let me tell you this, Fred." He looked up, surprised at the scratchy roughness in her voice. "I know you don't care, I know that these money matters are—too—mundane for you. But let me tell you this, Fred. Eleanor must have her chance. I intend to save every penny of what we get from *that*"—she tossed her head to the ceiling, stiffened, and her hands twisted together as if she were drawing herself up to some great height—"and if you stand in my way I'll leave you." Now she turned and went toward the bedroom.

My father looked after her, and then stood up, holding his thick brown book. "Your mother is strangely excitable," he said to me. "She may possibly have a thyroid disease. Undoubtedly due to some lack in our drinking water." He left the room. I heard his heavy step go down the stairs. For minutes I stared at the painting across the room before it actually came into focus, a silly horn spilling dead fruit, and then I put down my book. I took a crumpled cigarette from the pack my father had left and lit it and walked around the room straightening. It was as messed as if blows had been struck. The pillows were dented; my mother's scissors, cloth, and thread, my father's papers scattered. Then I heard the bedroom door open and my mother came out. She went toward the kitchen. She wore her coat and the punched-in velour hat and I thought, with a kind of numb wonder, she's going to Schaeffer. I went to the window and lifted the blind. Beyond the glass there was no traffic and no one was walking. Streets and sidewalks were evenly drifted, like an open field. On the windowsill outside were two miniature slopes of snow and in the light of the street lamp that beamed on a level with this window the snow whirled, not white but red and gold, like sparks struck from an anvil. Nothing seemed white. The night air was brown, the snow red and gold. I heard a scraping sound and in a moment my mother appeared below dragging a shovel. The wind blew and pulled at her coat. She balanced the shovel against her, took off her hat, squashed it down into her coat pocket, and began shoveling. The wind blew, showers of gold snow sparks whirled, and I watched my mother, a small black figure, with sparks blowing around her, digging, lifting, tossing cold fire from the slag that the roaring cauldron of the night rained down upon her and a pain, not red or blue, but phosphorescent, green, burned in back of my ribs. I knew the awful week was over, but it was my father, not myself, who had paid.

10

Every day, even this Sunday before Christmas, my mother gets out of bed quickly, dresses quickly, and starts working at breakfast. Still, despite her deftness, it's as if something were out of gear. She says hardly a word before ten; her tongue seems locked in the frozen waste of her motions. Breakfast represents for her that series of exercises she must go through to arrive at the limber sanity of midmorning. My father, on the other hand, wakes up bungling and chatty. Normally, he arises at ten, but something about Sunday, the challenging quiet, I think, propels him upward at eight. Today he is reading *The New York Times*. I hear from the kitchen the sounds of my mother's pans banging, the fuzzy voice of a radio choir, and above all this, my father. He reads loudly but not continuously, skims with a mumbling buzz those words and sections not crucial to content, and supplies instead his own commentary.

"Case number twenty-three, who was found living in an unheated cellar—my God, think of that—at age eighty-one, L.J. has no living relatives—don't doubt it—and hmmmmmmm—living on a diet of—you wonder how some people hang on, this would have long ago killed me—toast and milk—but—aha!—too weak to climb the stairs out of his apartment, he—hmmm . . ."

This morning, I dress slowly, swimming wantonly in Sunday time and sunlight. It's absolutely delightful to dress in sunshine. Off and on, for days now, snow has been falling, and even when it stops the sky above it hangs swollen and gray, as if exhausting itself in an unproductive labor. Now sunshine explodes in the room and my friend, the nymph in the mirror, moves in a mist of gold light. Still shoeless, in a white slip, she lifts her hairbrush, strokes, and her hair shakes fire. What is it about shoelessness that makes for innocence? She looks like a mountain girl, flat-footed, round calfed. But putting on shoes changes roles, in slip and high heels becomes something out of a movie on lower-class life, a hip-tossing, brassy-haired doll. She clicks, swivel-hipped, to the closet, rejects the Quaker gray, the patched plaid, the lumpy maroon, and chooses a bold blue, an electric blue, the color of her mood. I lift it, and it falls, crackling, around me. My mother knocks once and walks in.

"Your breakfast is on the table," she says, and I see, puzzled, that she is still in pajamas. She moves slowly toward the bed, then sits on its edge and cautiously lies back. I don't ever remember seeing my mother sick, at least not enough to be in bed, and I take it as a good sign that she still has her shoes on—laceless, square-toed, square-heeled shoes she wears instead of slippers.

"What's the matter?" I ask. "Aren't you feeling well?"

She covers her eyes with her arm as if in embarrassment and asks me will I kindly take her offering to church. I ask, can I get tea? An aspirin? No no, she says, she'll feel better soon, it's just a cold. But her voice is dry and tired with an odd leaflike rustling in it. I go to the bed. Stubbornly, her legs still dangle, but I cover her with the comforter, and pull down the blinds, diminishing the sun to quivering strips. Are you sure there's nothing? I ask, but she whispers no, and I leave the room, closing the door softly.

In the kitchen my father is drinking sassafras tea and frowning at the paper. The choir, a local group, it seems, has become enmired in the paths of "We Three Kings." I reach over my father's head to the wall shelf and turn down the blare.

"Good morning," he says, not looking up. "I trust you slept well."

"Nn," I say, answering the same Sunday question I've been getting for years. Standing, I pour a half cup of coffee and drink it.

"Why is it," he asks, "that you can't sit down to enjoy breakfast like the rest of the world?"

"I'm late," I say. "Listen, Father, don't you think Mother's sick? She's in bed."

He lifts his brows. "Listen to this: 'Over ninety per cent of the school children of Chile—' Is she actually in bed?"

"Not really *all* in bed. I mean, she's down on it."

"I see. Well, that's bad, but not *that* bad. Your mother's got a remarkable constitution. I wish I had it. I don't know what you've got. I've a feeling you've inherited mine."

"Do you think she needs aspirin?"

"I have given her aspirin, thank you." He half rises in

his chair and turns the awful music up again. "If you're going to church hadn't you better leave soon? The main event is about to begin."

"You're not going?"

"Next week is my week," he says, and I shrug and take a square of burnt sienna toast and get my coat and go downstairs.

Outside the air is startling, sharp and light, with a clear, menthol aftertaste. My nostrils stick closed. The sun bounces at me, a hard, bright ball in the bitter, blue plain of sky. Across the street two or three icicles hanging from the pseudo-classical cornice of the Warren Hotel wink lewdly at me like an old man's teeth. I smile. Cold before Christmas always seems cheerful and people in the streets don't have the grim look they acquire in January. Where did Stephen say he'd park? My mother would have a fit if she knew I saw him on Sunday morning. I start walking up toward St. Vincent's. Going past me, downstream, the Sunday tide is sober, dark-clothed, well-behaved, headed where I should be going, toward the solid stone portals of First Presbyterian. Upstream, toward the gilded, smoky, pungent interior of St. Vin's, the crowd is colorful, jaunty, and gay; the girls wear jingling lapel ornaments decked with ribbons and walk to church on their boyfriends' arms. Ardyce Flather, driving her mother's Buick, leans out of the window to offer me a lift. When I decline she shakes her head. I walk up the block, past the Medical Arts Building, past the Junior High School, and cross the street at the corner. Coming out of St.

Vincent's I see Fran Patchoulis and Nancy Rourke framed in a pergola of blue, and I wave and walk on, and then just past the Fulton Ford place I see the car, smoking like a warmed black egg. He has the motor running and, I hope, the heater. A domestic cloud of brown smoke trails from the tail of the little house. At the car window, I rub a clearing in the frost and wave through it and then slide into the humming warmth. By way of greeting, I put my frosted glove fingers on his cheek. He winces and takes my hand.

"I walked a million miles for one of your smiles," I say and lean toward him. We kiss, well-practiced now, but shyly, because we kiss, unnaturally, in sunshine. His face has a tender, just shaved look, and he smells faintly spicy, like a young tree. He has a thick maroon sweater on over a white shirt and tie.

"You're all dressed up," I say, "did you go to church?"

"Sure," he says, "just now."

"Well, that's out of the way," I say.

"Sure," he says. We never talk about religion but he's good about my teasing. I don't know what he really thinks, but I guess that he goes to get it over with and doesn't pray too hard.

"Should I take you over now?" he asks.

"To church?" I say. "Not today. There's no point, I forgot my mother's offering. Look at all this sun! Isn't it gorgeous? Where shall we go?"

"You mean your mother isn't going to church?" He looks worried. He doesn't understand my tendency not to tell my mother where I am.

"She's got a cold and isn't going. And my father only

goes on Christmas. To keep his hand in, he says. Rochester! Buffalo! We could drive out to the lake and walk on the ice."

He looks anxiously at the dashboard and I see now that the arrow of the fuel gauge is just a microinch off E. "The thing is," he says, "I got to get to Albany tonight on a buck. I tried to borrow five from Mike last night and he flipped me a single, the spender."

I sigh, unlatch my purse, and scramble around among lipstick, compact, Kleenex, broken comb, and bobby pins. My wallet I know has nothing but three thin dimes. "Listen, can't we just ride around downtown? Just to go somewhere. I don't want to go back home."

"I've been downtown before," he says, "but all right," and shifts and we start. We've gone about ten blocks, just past the Clifton General Hospital, when the red needle quivers and leaps suddenly not to E but past it.

"Hot damn," he says, "now we've had it." He pulls up to the curb and we meditate.

"We can't just sit here," I say. As if absorbing our gloom the bright blue air becomes vague; in the left-hand corner of the windshield I see a bomb-shaped cloud covering the sun.

"Rosie and Mike were out to four or five, to a wedding or something."

I look at his profile, hooked so hopelessly over the wheel.

"We could go up to my place," he says, "and do some math." He looks straight ahead and I don't know what to say. "They always sleep late, until two or three."

"If you think it'll be all right," I say, and we drive up to the Crab Street Esso and get a dollar's worth of gas and then drive up the hill and east, to Stephen's.

I have not been in his room before. It is on the third floor of the Wojcik's narrow house and its view is that of the houses behind. From the street these buildings present a solid front of dirty red brick, but it is here, from the rear, that their patchy indignities show. The wooden back porches are painted mongrel colors, yellow or tan or gray. The house just opposite is the worst with a gray porch which years ago began to erupt in blisters. There is a clothesline strung across the porch and on it a pair of frozen work pants. In the scanty yard two thin, short-haired dogs, a brown and a black, yank and snarl and run, tugging at another length of clothesline that attaches them to the railing of the porch. Their goal is a loaded garbage pail placed just beyond their reach near the chicken-wire fence. They plow through the urine-spotted snow toward it, and are continually surprised when the line snaps them to. I let the curtain drop and turn from the window.

"Who are your back neighbors?" I ask Stephen.

"Old man Kabochek and his crazy wife. They're tighter than ticks. Never give those mutts anything to eat. The dogs run around like that all the time. They used to drive me nuts when I'd study up here. I'd go down to the corner and buy some Milk-Bones to throw at 'em just to shut 'em up. Old man Kabochek raised hell, said I was trying to poison his dogs." Stephen is sitting on the edge of his unmade bed flipping through some of his back quizzes and looking through the algebra text. He mumbles to himself. "Hey. What'd you do on trinomials?"

"Was that October?" I ask.

"I guess so, yeah."

"I must have failed that, I don't remember. Is that the stuff with three equations?"

"Cut it out," he says. "Yeah, here it is, page eighty-four. You want to look at this?"

I go over and sit carefully a foot away from him on the edge of the bed. While he culls the problem, I look around the room. It's very messy. The bed, a kind of large cot, needs clean sheets, and the green wool blanket has lost its binding. The bureau drawers leak underwear at the corners. Oil smudges set off the tan stripes of the wallpaper and the room's main ornament, a tall, sad radiator, seems to be out of condition, for the room is quite cold.

"What's the matter?" he asks. He holds his cigarette between thumb and forefinger, watching me.

"I don't know. Have you always lived here, in this house?"

"Sure. Why?"

"I was just thinking about—"

"What?"

"Nothing."

He tips his ash into a Pepsi bottle half full of butts and looks vaguely around. "I guess I should have picked up a little, huh?"

"We shouldn't be up here."

"Once Rosie gets up we wouldn't get anything done downstairs."

"She's not up yet," I say.

"She'll get hungry pretty soon," he says. "Then she'll go down for food and put it on a tray and take it back upstairs. That's the way they spend Sundays. Staying in bed."

"All day?"

"Yeah."

"My God, what ever for?"

He laughs. "I don't know," he says, "you think about it. You want to start with this problem?"

Our heads bend to the book. I explain to him how I would solve the equation and he laughs. He explains how he solved it and I don't understand it at all. I sigh and sit up straight.

"Now what," he says.

"I can't think," I say. "This room's so messy."

"What do you want, a dustcloth?"

I stand up and go to the window and pull back the limp curtain. "Stephen? What do you think of my mother?"

"Your mother? Geez, I don't know. She's all right. She's your mother."

"No, honestly."

"I don't know. I guess she's smart. Yeah, she knows a lot."

"Do you think she's happy?"

"I never thought about it. All I know is, she hates my guts."

"How do you know that?"

"Doesn't she?"

"Not really. It's not you, it's everything."

"Everything else and me too."

"She thinks I've changed. I used to read a lot more, and work harder in school."

"You still work too hard."

"Why do you always say that?"

"Because it makes you so mad."

I stick my tongue out at him and bend to look at the magazines he has lined up in stacks between the bed and wall. *Popular Mechanics, Popular Science,* some school library issues of *Scientific American,* and a couple of things called *Man,* which, strangely, have only near-naked females on their covers. I hold up a magazine showing a girl in pink underpants lying on a bearskin rug.

"A great library," I say, "of dirty pictures."

He smacks the math book shut and tosses it across the room. It hits a knob of his dresser and flops, a thing in pain, to the floor and he flops back flat on the bed and puts a hand under his head and smokes.

"Shit," he says bitterly to the spotted ceiling.

"Now what," I say, mocking him.

"Go to hell," he says. This makes me smile. I sit down next to him and start very gently playing the piano on his ribs.

"Cut it out," he says.

"Name this song," I say.

"No," he says, and sits up and drops the cigarette into the Pepsi bottle. "You don't give a damn, do you?"

"About what?" I ask, folding my hands in my lap and laughing at him. But he is serious.

"About me."

His eyes are narrowed, so dense they seem black. He leans toward me until his face is against mine, and I feel the whisk of his lashes as his eyes close. We sit very still with our faces together, and he leans against me, without kissing me, and then after a while pulls me slowly down next to him on the bed. He keeps his arms around me and doesn't open his eyes. I feel him shiver.

"Stephen?" I ask. "Are you cold?"

He shakes his head no, and then says, "Kiss me, Ellie, all right?"

I kiss him, his mouth all loose and tasting of the cigarette and then he half turns and kisses me. We lie there turned to each other, our faces close, our mouths together but not kissing, and then he begins again.

"Ellie?" he says, and his hands slip under my clothes.

"No," I say, "don't, I can't."

"Why? Do you love me? All right, shhh."

"No, listen, no."

"All right, then, just . . ."

"I don't."

"Ellie, for God's sake, then just hold me" and his hand closes around mine and takes it down to where he is: stiff, turgid, hot, and his hand keeps mine there, and he begins.

It was all so strange. I hadn't thought it was anything like that, a great push of stuff, and later he shivered in my arms as if he were sick or cold. We slept. In my sleep I heard the radiators knock and when I woke up the sky was a heavy gray, the room warm. My head ached. I sat up and began buttoning my dress. He rolled over and smiled up at me shyly, a new bridegroom smile, then stood up and started to tuck in his shirt.

"The way I figure it out, we can get married in two years."

I looked out the window and saw that it had begun to snow again, large feather-shaped flakes. How true was it, I wondered, that each one is different? Amazing. You wondered why. Oh, accident, of course. Who cared about single crystals? As a little kid, four or five, I'd sit in the snow watching the navy-blue shoulder of my snowsuit, where doomed flakes lighted and lived that instant before they dissolved. It had seemed sad, their going so fast. All these careless endeavors of the earth. Every snowflake different as a sperm, all sperms endlessly unlike, billions of singular eggs, and chance combinations of the two, making ad infinitum variety, per collision, per pair. Old Mother Earth. Coarse, filthy bawd in the window, indifferently picking her scalp, she lazily watches her children who romp below, in the gutter.

"What's the matter, don't you believe in marriage?" He pulled the maroon sweater over his head and arranged it on his hips in a neat line.

"In two years?" I said. "That's crazy. How could we ever get married in college?"

"I don't know, we could work it out. Couldn't you be a

secretary or something? You know Jack Mercer? He went to Cornell and met this girl up there and got married. She works in the Admissions' Office."

"How could I be a secretary and go to college at the same time?"

He looked at me perplexed. "You wouldn't have to go if we got married. I mean, what for?" He shrugged and winked. "You can be educated without going to college, Eleanor." But I didn't smile and his face changed. "Well, geez, look at your mother. She's educated, isn't she? She never went."

"That's why she wants me to go, she doesn't think she is."

"Hell, Ellie, how much do you need?"

"God knows. Sometimes I feel so stupid."

"The trouble is that you're not."

"There are things I can't figure out for myself. Why does everything seem so wasteful? Why is there so much of everything? Sometimes I can't stand the world. Plants, insects, animals, people—we're all jostling each other. No one counts. We live and die in chunks. Then it's over—dead and forgotten."

"You haven't forgotten your brother."

"My brother? You know how I remember him? Before the end of the war I saw a newsreel, no, it was earlier, in the fall, and I thought I saw Louis in it. Soldiers were moving across the fields. The trees were bare, the ground covered with leaves. They passed a dead soldier lying on the ground. His face was turned toward the side, and it looked as if he had a piece of dirt wrapped in his hand. Behind me some idiot said, 'That's a Kraut, all right.' Whenever I think: *Louis*—he's what I think of first. Funny, because my brother was killed later on. It couldn't have been him at all."

He was standing next to the bureau, leaning against it. Now he found a loose knob and spun it. "I believe that when you die your soul is still alive. Somehow. A spark you can't put out. If you were a Catholic you'd believe that, too."

"I'm not, though."

"I know it."

"I never will be either."

"I guess not."

"Don't you care?"

"I don't know. I think it's nice if a girl's religious. For the kids and all that. I guess I'd like the girl I marry to be Catholic."

"I couldn't ever marry a strong Catholic, Stephen."

This made him smile. "I'm not a strong anything," he said.

I walked around to where he was standing and pulled my coat off the chair.

"Are you mad?" he asked.

"Why?"

"Not at me? About today?"

"You're silly. No."

"Really?"

"Yes."

181

"You lie so much I never know when to believe you." He looked at me soberly, then put his arm around my shoulders and we went downstairs. In the kitchen he made peanut-butter sandwiches, whistling and diddling while I watched, then sat next to me and coaxed me to eat tiny bites. We laughed and stickily, in between bites, kissed each other.

But I hadn't told him what I'd wanted to. Stephen? It isn't death that scares me—I've been dying off and on for years. It's life. Everyday, ordinary life.

II

When I got home the house was dark. There were no lights on, not even in the bedroom. In the kitchen, when I pressed the switch, things sprang into an oily yellow still life, but exactly as I'd seen them that morning: the ransacked *Times* in crumpled peaks and plains, my father's crumb-spattered plate, his teacup full of dregs, my curdled coffee. I dumped the coffee in the sink and put away the butter. Then I heard a bump in the hall and turned. My mother, still in her bathrobe and pajamas, was standing in the doorway. Her face was flushed and her eyes had a bright, sly look. She laughed at me.

"What time is it?" she asked in a thick voice and looked up at the kitchen clock. "Why, it's early." For what, I wondered, staring, then caught her as she staggered forward and half fell against me. I helped her to a chair. She sat down carefully, clinging with both hands to the chair back.

"What is it?" I asked, frightened.

She shook her head and coughed. The cough made a harsh grinding sound as if a giant drill were boring down between her lungs. Her face twisted in pain.

"Where did Daddy go?" I asked when she had stopped.

She pursed her lips and looked at me wickedly. "Movies," she whispered, with that same strange merry look. Then the downstairs door slammed, and I heard my father's step.

"Hello!" he called from the living room. "Anyone home? Hello!" He came into the kitchen and tossed his hat so that it slid the length of the counter. "Don't anyone go to the Alhambra this week, it's not worth free admission."

My mother laughed. My father looked down at her in surprise, complimented by this rare appreciation. Then his brows lifted. "My God," he said to me, "it's almost five o'clock. Don't tell me your mother's been lounging in her nightwear all day."

"She's sick," I said, "really sick," and as if to prove it, she had a chill so violent that her teeth rattled and the chair she sat on shook. When it was over, her face took on an astonished, docile look. My father incredulous, started at a run out of the kitchen, then yelled over his shoulder at me to get my mother to bed. By the time I had, he had come back with his black bag. He waved me out of the bedroom and shut the door. In a few minutes he came out and went to the telephone in the living room.

"Hello!" he yelled at it. "Hello! Oh, Marjorie, this is Fred Munson. Is Harvey—he is—that's fine—hello, Harvey, this is Fred Munson. It's Frieda, I'm afraid she's pretty sick. Pneumonia. I thought I'd take her down to the General. I'd appreciate your coming in, if you could . . . Do you want to call—oh, good, all right, I'll see you there. Thank you. Yes, yes. Good-bye."

We didn't even get her dressed. She was as limp and cumbersome as an oversize doll and her eyes had a doll's stiff flicker. I got her coat and all we could do was stuff her arms into it, then bundle the blanket around her and lace the Red Cross shoes.

"Come on now, Frieda," my father said, "up, up we go. Careful, that's right, lean on me." We were as far as the bedroom door when she began another cough, her shoulders hunched against the pain. My father dug into his overcoat pocket and brought up a handkerchief. "Spit it up," he said, cupping it in front of her mouth. She spat a glob of sticky red fluid. He examined it curiously, then wadded it into his pocket. "Good girl," he said cheerfully. Slowly, we worked our way through the house and down the stairs. Outside in the black bitter air she stopped to cough again and I felt that under the wadding of the blanket she was slippery, amorphous, determined to elude me. We half carried her into the car and in the front seat she slumped back, exhausted. My father drove slowly and carefully the thirteen city blocks to the hospital. There they were waiting for us. From among the other patients she was plucked like some special flower. A nurse pushed a wheel chair toward her, she was pressed down into it, and they set off, my father at a half-run after the wheel chair, down the slick-floored, narrowing brown tunnel of a corridor to the corner, where, in the eerie red glow of an exit light, they turned and were gone.

. . . . .

185

The last time I was in this hospital I was eleven and had appendicitis. Then there was something templelike about the waiting room—space in it was cloudy and vast, floated, as in the U.S. Capitol rotunda. Light filtered in and down through dusty clerestory windows. The blue-gray walls, the hard, faintly creaking wooden chairs drawn up against these walls, the dark-brown linoleum, and the iron-faced nurse who sat at twelve o'clock in the large, round room all gave this place an air of portentuousness. Beyond this outer room white-robed priests went on about their rites and ministrations. Those waiting talked softly, seldom read, and the harshest noise was the turning of chart notes on the nurse's clipboard. When I left the hospital, loaded with toys and get-well cards and a letter from the seventh grade, I saw a man sitting here at the bottom of a dusty well of sunlight, crying.

Now it is all different, all noise and cheer. There is no daylight. A false ceiling has been put in, and day and night, tubes of bluish light hum and fluoresce. Walls have been constructed to put an edge on the lofty space. Now we face the possibilities of death sitting on orange molded-plastic chairs, in a square beige and green box. There is no nurse on duty here. The tall, green potted plants are so unnaturally bright they seem to be made of plastic too, and across from where I sit broods a wall full of machines: cigarettes, candy, gum, crackers, and three kinds of soft drinks, each one a dime. Everyone eats, smokes or chews, rustles, hacks, scrapes and shuffles. The man across from me reads a comic book. When a nurse comes in the whole room looks up, interested, as her money clinks down the gullet of a cigarette machine, and the machine hiccoughs and gives up a mint-green pack. Filter tips. At the same time, Dr. McLeod comes through the door and the nurse looks at him and smiles and he raises a big red hand, then walks quickly down the hall. My father, looking small, comes from the opposite direction to meet him. They go down the hall together, McLeod striding, my father walking so fast he seems to limp. I wait twenty-five minutes before my father comes back. He does not even look for me but goes into one of the doors marked Laboratory. I wonder if I should wait, or if he remembers I'm here, so I get up and go to the same door and knock and walk in.

"That's it, Miss Tresnewski," my father is saying. "If you'd work on it as soon as the sample comes in."

Miss Tresnewski, in a starchy white lab coat, is filing her nails and looks up sullenly over my father's shoulder at me. "Swell," she says. She does not pick up the yellow slips of paper he has placed on the laboratory table.

"You think you could do them—quite soon?" my father asks.

"I'll try," she says. She puts down her emery board and picks up the slips. She studies them, then reads them off, loudly and painfully, as if the writing were very hard to read.

"You want a white count, right?"

"Yes."

"A—what?—oh, a differential. And a hematocrit."

"Yes."

"And a sputum culture, and a gram stain, right?"

"That's right, yes."

"You know what, Dr. Munson? Today's Sunday and I'm supposed to be out of here by six on Sundays."

"It's not six yet, Miss Tresnewski."

"Uh-huh. It's five forty-five."

"This is a very sick patient. These tests are very important."

"They're all sick, Dr. Munson. Listen, I don't mean to be fresh or anything, but you know what this place pays me? To come in here on Sundays? I could make out better in Kresge's. And then half the time I got to stay two-three hours late. This F. Munson a relative of yours?"

Gradually, my father's face had been hardening into a weary clay color. "No," he said, "not technically. Not that it matters. I'd like the work done, and as soon as possible." I coughed. He turned and blinked at me. "Oh, Eleanor," he said, "I didn't know you were still here."

I asked if I should go.

"Yes," he said, "of course. There's nothing you can do here, unless you'd like to read some slides." He smiled at Miss Tresnewski, she stared sulkily at me, and he walked past me out of the door, only nodding to me as he passed, as if I were some rather distant kin.

At home by seven, I found I was very tired. I lay down on my bed and smoked a number of cigarettes, one after the other. My bones ached as if they were draining marrow.

Above me our new tenant, Miss Ryan, made her small domestic noises, like a pack rat in its papers. She was a timid, neat person who had been, for forty-two years, a court stenographer. She went out to mass early in the morning and came back about the time I left for school, with a small brown sack of groceries. Give us this day our daily. She was afraid, living in our house, and had asked my mother if it were possible for young hoodlums to come down over the roof and get into her bedroom. My mother had promised to sprinkle broken glass on the roof. When Miss Ryan had gone, my mother turned to me and said, rolling her eyes, "In *her* bedroom!"

The truth was my mother had always been very brave. Sounds at night didn't frighten her; it was my mother who killed the bugs in the house. She hunted moths with an upraised broom and once (on the night of Sully's junior high school graduation, when we were sitting in a booth in The Garden Restaurant) she stabbed to death with a forefinger the cockroach that had come scuttling across the wall toward us.

My cigarettes made me woozy and I stubbed out the fourth. In the dark, without the bulky rise of her shape, my mother's bed seemed to accuse me. She believed me to be lost. She had nurtured me toward a brilliant bloom and instead, like a simple weed, I craved simple things. For what, her incessant daily care, doses of love, discipline and hope? Lost, all lost. And what, besides my future, did she have? Monotony of daily life, endless tasks, instead of love my father's weird complaints. Nothing. Nothing, nothing,

nothing . . . nothing . . . no . . . thing . . . and now . . . what's this? where am I? alone at the top of a dangerous hill, and where are the other children? all gone home. It is very dark, but despite what they say I will, I know I can (can you?), and I take my sled and throw it under me and—there—feel a dreadful flare of danger, the crystal wind sings in my ears and the cold in my mouth tastes bitter and—faster—do you see way down—faster—there where I am heading? where the lights of that house—so fast—spread orange squares on the blue snow? Too fast, too fast! But silly, it's all right, you can stop, this is seven or eight years ago, and I lurched, caught myself, and woke up frightened.

Yes, years ago. That night (it's all right, years ago) when I came home, I heard about old Mrs. Hansen's dying, in the farmhouse whose lights I had seen over the hill. My father had been there. He and I arrived home together but had come by different routes. My mother had cocoa and tomato soup for me and my father's tea ready. In the living room Sully and Louis bantered—eternal, idle malice—and listened in between to Jack Benny. My father spread orange-streaked wartime margarine on his toast and my mother, watching him, said, "Oh, come now, Fred, you've known for months she was going to die."

Under the tomato soup, the edge of my spoon had a dull metallic flavor.

"She didn't want to go," my father said, and his knife clattered to the table. In the living room Jack Benny's footsteps echoed as he went down the long stone steps to his vault. "She didn't want to go," he insisted. "You'd be amazed how they don't want to die, even the old ones and the ones in pain. She held my hand and one minute she was there and the next she was—a stone."

I looked up and my father's remembering face had a shiny, petrified look.

My mother shrugged and lifted her coffee cup. "Seventy-eight. And the thousands of boys who are dying in this war."

"Daddy," I asked, "what makes you die?"

"Don't be foolish," my mother said sharply to me.

"No," I said. "I mean, how do you?"

My father's face thawed with the relief of thought. "A very good scientific question," he said. "You see, the heart stops pumping blood and the blood, carrying oxygen, does not circulate. Therefore, the cells die. I suppose you might say it was—uh—suffocation."

My mother brought her cup down with a clink. "How interesting," she said dryly. "But think of all those living cells that might as well be dead. They make up the people who *should* be. What I've learned is that you can suffocate and be alive, too. Is it the Hippocratic Oath, Fred, that makes you think death is never a blessing?"

My mother's empty bed now seemed a sign. In her view death was the end of life and you accepted this. What worried me now was her resignation. My father struggled with death daily. He woke up in the morning scrubbing death from his eyelids—*cogito ergo sum, ergo, sum*. His thinking, that whirring, cockeyed machine, seemed the thing by which he proved himself alive. An illness of his would not have been so dangerous. I put my face in the pillow and wished for my mother (not even now could I bring myself to blaspheme by prayer) and wished that, despite my poor father, if it would make her happy, to let her marry Schaeffer. If, I thought, she would only get well.

12

My father, sitting across from me on the other side of the yellow formica-topped table, has reset his silver twice, drunk the water from his tumbler all at once, and now tries both to read the blurred blue type of the plastic-faced menu and to find the start of the tricky red cellophane tape that binds a package of saltines. Our waitress, tight-faced and orange-haired, looks bored. Tonight, Tuesday, is The Garden's slow night. There aren't many customers. Across the aisle and one booth down, two old ladies sit huddled and pecking over their specials. In the rear booth three men smoke cigars and play cards noisily. Waiting, our waitress shows us her flattish profile and taps her pencil on the order pad.

"Hmm," my father says, "I think I'll have the Salisbury steak. Is that broiled or fried, do you know, Miss?"

She gives him a wan look. "You want it broiled?"

"Yes. Also, I do not want the peas. At least not as they are. Do you have puréed peas?"

"Puréed? You mean all mashed up?"

"That's right, yes." My father rewards her with a smile. The waitress's eyebrows, dark, penciled arcs, twitch. "I'll have to see. You want the salad?"

"Salad? No. What else is—beets, no, corn, no; what kind of potatoes did you say?"

"French fry."

"Oh. Do you have any rice?"

"It's not on the dinner, Mac. I'll have to ask."

"I'll have the rice as long as it's not too dry. That is, not granular."

"I'll have the number two," I get in quickly. The waitress inserts her pencil inside the rubber band that holds together the order pad, and swings away toward the kitchen. In the rear booth the men applaud her coming.

"Take it easy, fellas, huh?" she says, and shoves into the kitchen doors. They swing apart and a cloud of steam, a clank, a roar, roll out as if from a minor hell. My father has at last unsnagged the red tape and begins eating crackers.

"It's amazing," he says, "how many people have asked for your mother. She's been sick since Sunday, only two days, and at least ten people have called. She's gotten several cards and many flowers. And she thinks she has no friends in this town. The Ladies' Aid sent flowers and the Physicians' Wives and Mr. and Mrs. Byers. And Mrs. Littrell. You know Mrs. Littrell, don't you, Eleanor? I always did think she was a nice person, if stupid. And you remember the carpenter who did the third floor, the one who came to dinner on Thanksgiving?"

"He owns a construction company, Father," I say. "He's really not just a carpenter."

"What's wrong with being a carpenter? One of the most honorable of trades. I'm merely identifying the man. What was his name? Schubert? Schuman? Something Germanic."

"Schaeffer."

"Right! Damnedest thing, he came by the hospital today. Came to see your mother and brought her a dozen roses. Red, beautiful things. I thought that was awfully nice. Probably had nothing to do with the fact that your mother just sent him a check for four hundred and some dollars. He's probably quite a decent person, don't you think so?"

I nod, agreeing. The waitress comes and slides our plates toward us as if holding them offends her. My father's plate has on it Salisbury steak, a small mound of rice, and a jar of Baby Peas. He looks at the dish and frowns, unscrews the cap of the jar, peers into it and pours Baby Peas over the rice.

"Still," he says, stirring the mixture with his fork, "I couldn't let him go in to see her. I'd expected some change today, yet—" He doesn't finish the sentence, begins instead to prod his meat.

I ask, "What does Dr. McLeod think?"

"Think? What do you mean, think? It's pneumonia, of course. It's simply that in penicillin therapy you expect a response in seventy-two hours. Generally. Of course there might be complications. The heart business."

This startles me. "What's wrong with Mother's heart?"

"Nothing, yet. She had rheumatic fever as a child and recovered except for a weak valve. Gives her a slight murmur. You see, instead of the heart going bum-BOOM, bum-BOOM, bum-BOOM"—he calls this out and taps the rhythm for me on the edge of the table and the two old ladies look up with bright, startled eyes—"it goes bum-BOOM-pshhh, bum-BOOM-pshhh, bum-BOOM-pshhh. Normally, that's all right, there's nothing much wrong with that. But in pneumonia the bugs like to settle on that damaged spot. They dig in, entrench themselves in the heart's lining, and then there's trouble."

"But that hasn't happened yet?"

"I don't know. I don't think so. There aren't any other signs, except the fact that she hasn't yet made any definite progress."

Behind my father The Garden's revolving door spins and stops and Stephen's father, natty and pink-faced, steps in. He hails the cashier and she lifts her moon face from her magazine. "Hi ya, Mike hon," she says. He waves and passes her Alcatraz of chewing gum, mints, cigarettes, cigars, tobacco, and comes down the aisle toward us. I feel myself blushing but he only winks at me and as he passes our booth squeezes my father's shoulder.

"Hi, Doc!" he yells. My father looks up, then around the corner of the booth.

"Who—oh, hello Wojcik," he says and goes back to his green-stained rice.

I begin nervously to butter a roll. "I didn't know you knew him," I say.

"Who, Wojcik? Why, I know all Clifton's major criminals," my father says. "From my nights on police duty. Wojcik's supposed to be a rich man."

"But he couldn't be," I say as my father looks up. "That's Stephen's father."

"You mean your friend Stephen? Oh, yes, I'd forgotten what his last name was." My father leans out of the booth again and looks down the aisle. Wojcik has arrived at the boisterous last booth but instead of sitting down in it has pulled over a chair, so that he is planted squarely in front of the kitchen doors. As we watch the waitress comes swinging out of the kitchen with a tray full of food. The tray tilts, the dishes slide and she screams.

"Hey, hey," the men cry, pleased.

"For Chris' sake, Mike," the waitress says, but she has saved the plates from spilling. As she serves the men Wojcik casually puts an arm around her hips and tweaks the strings of her apron. She jerks away.

"Not here, Mike," one of the men yells. I turn back to my father.

"I don't think Mr. Wojcik could be rich, Daddy," I say. "He never gives Stephen any money."

"These Polish people are often very sparing," my father says. "You'd be surprised, though, how much real estate some of them own. They like to buy land."

"I don't think the Wojciks own anything except their house," I say.

"You may be right," my father says. "He gambles himself, I hear. It's a bad thing when a man has the vices of his profession."

The noise from the back booth grows louder and more hilarious. We eat in silence. My father cleans his plate, in fact, scrapes it, and in a concession to what he thinks are Clifton manners, crosses his knife and fork upon it. He stares toward the rear.

"So that's your friend's father," he says.

"Stephen's not a bit like him," I say.

"One nice thing about being an offspring is that you are not held responsible for the action of your elders. So you say Stephen's not a chip off the old block, eh? No, I can see he isn't—yet. Though who knows where the devious paths of heredity lead? He's a senior in high school, you say?"

"A junior," I correct.

"He isn't in your year?" my father asks, surprised.

"We're both juniors, Daddy," I say, stretching my patience.

"You are?" my father says. "Oh, yes, of course. Hmm. Now, I understand that the elder Wojcik is awfully clever. I suppose he could be rich if he didn't gamble. Stephen probably got his aptitude for numbers from his father—I'm sure gambling must involve an inherent love of mathematics. No, I think your friend's a nice fellow, really I do. The last time I saw him—the night you went to that dance—I had a puzzle for him, you know, one of those mathematical things, and we ran through it, the one about the five law clerks who lived in five identical houses—"

"I know, Daddy," I say. He had held us up twenty minutes saying, "Wait a minute, wait a minute, let's do this scientifically."

"I don't think I finished it," he says and begins extracting from his pockets a number of small bottles. He lines them up, unscrews each cap, unplugs the cotton stopper from each one, and dumps out pills into his cupped hand. The old ladies stare as he swallows all in one gulp, and then, as he smiles at them, they shyly duck their heads together.

"Time to go," he says. He repacks his medicine and stands up. We put on our coats. The waitress emerges from the rear booth, strips our bill from her pad and drops it on the table without looking at us. My father, without looking at the bill, reaches inside his coat for change and leaves two quarters under his plate. Outside, we find the car, parked as it characteristically is, at an angle four feet from the curb.

"Well," my father says, patting his pockets for the car keys, "that was a good meal. Now we'll see about your mother. I'm sure that tonight she'll be a great-deal-better." But he doesn't say anything more, and he drives so badly that the ride to the hospital is full of near-collisions.

My mother that night was just as she'd been the night before. Under the cellophane sides of the oxygen tent her face was still orchid gray. Her coughs shook the tent but did not wake her. I sat staring through the clear plastic flap, afraid that if she woke up she wouldn't know me. My father came in once and went out. A nurse came in, adjusted the valve on the tent, and went out. The radiators hissed. As the steam came on, Schaeffer's roses, nodding from a glass beaker on the night stand, seemed to unfold and their sweet, decadent smell rose with the warmth. At eight my father came in again with Dr. McLeod.

"I did order the whole new series," my father said, "and as you can see, it hasn't been done."

"I know, I know, I know," McLeod said. "I just checked the lab. Bare as a bone. Why the hell don't we hire a night technician?" He scratched the bristly back of his head. "I hate to ask you, Fred, but it's getting late and I've still got three patients to see . . ."

"No, no, no," my father said. "I was going to go over it anyway."

McLeod nodded and went out and then my father, without looking again at my mother, went through the door too. I followed him down the corridor and into the laboratory. He seemed not to know I was there. Inside the door he flipped the light switch and the fluorescent tubes buzzed and went on, laying out the lab like a math problem—flat white walls and the black solid cube of a lab table. My father went to a large, square aluminum box, bent down, opened the door, and looked inside like a woman watching a cake bake. He brought out a round glass dish.

"Agar," I said wisely.

"Umm," my father said, looking at it. Green shiny beads, like drops of lime Jello, were growing on the brown gel. He sniffed the dish and put it down on the counter, then went about the room assembling materials: slides, a wire loop, some bottles, and a paper bound book from the shelf over the lab's desk. He fiddled at the sink, then scraped the beads (now berry red) onto the slide and clipped the slide to the microscope's plate. He looked down into the microscope turning its knobs, then took off his glasses and looked at the slide again. Occasionally, he would look up at the blank wall. His face without glasses startled me. I so seldom saw him without them. He took baths with his glasses on and I remembered that years ago when we used (all of us) to go to the lake he had swum in an effective dog paddle with his chin well up like a spaniel's, and the glasses spotted with water and catching sun.

"Odd," he said.

"What?"

"Umm . . . I was thinking . . . how much I'd like to see your sister Sully."

"After mother gets well we could all go to California," I said brightly.

"Hmm . . . I was thinking that perhaps Sully might come here and bring the children. Your niece and nephew. Our—your mother's and my—grandchildren. I thought . . . it might give your mother a lift." He put on his glasses and turned to the index of the book, and then ruffled the book's pages. "Very curious . . . You see, if Sully did come, I'd like to offer to pay her way. What I mean is, I'm not so sure she would—or could—come if I didn't. I don't suppose, being a young couple, they've got much in the way of savings. Not that we have. What I mean to say is, the only savings we've got, really, is your college money."

He took off his glasses and looked at me, his face the unspectacled shy one. "What do you think of the idea?"

"Well, sure," I said, then blurted out crudely, ashamed of myself, "but what do I do about college?"

He put his glasses on. "Oh, I think we can work out a year. And your Uncle Herman Schlegel should be good for another year's credit. We'll try him, anyway, if you won't tell your mother. Then, it might be nice if you started thinking about your schoolwork. There are such things as scholarships, but as a rule they don't like to give them to students who fail. Ah, well, Eleanor! Why all this fuss? In five years you'll be married and have three children."

That made me laugh. "What makes you think so?"

"It's a law of nature. Pretty girls get married and married women tend to have children."

It took me a minute to understand he was talking about me, that he thought I was pretty. This made me feel different, not like Eleanor at all, but frivolous, like any pretty girl. I tilted my head and smiled.

"Now, Father, don't you think I'd be a better mother if I had a college education?" He was pawing the book again, running his finger down the index.

"What? Oh hokum. Anyone with the right sort of equipment can be a mother. Education will only make you nervous."

"Well, then," I said in exasperation, for having been complimented on my looks, I wanted also to be told I was bright, "what's the point of my going?"

"I have no idea," he said. "You tell me. If you really want to *learn* you can do so at home. Use the Clifton Public Library and save us a great deal of money. The only honest reason I have is that your mother wants you to go. You know," he said to the microscope, "you are a very strange bug. I haven't seen anything like you in—" he sat up straight. "My God, not in years. What was it Miss Tresnewski called you? E. coli? Ha! Klebsiella! It's Klebsiella!" and he jumped up and ran to the door.

"What's wrong?" I asked, but he was gone, half running, half limping down the hall. I went to the microscope and looked down and adjusted the knobs until the streaks jumped into focus. Klebsiella looked all right to me. I went to the bookshelf that was clamped over the lab's desk and took down an orange book I recognized—I had borrowed our copy from my father the year before when I did my A report on thyroid diseases. I looked up Klebsiella in the index. Then, on page four hundred seventy-one, under Klebsiella Pneumonia, I read:

When untreated, the mortality in acute cases averages about eighty per cent.

But my mother was being treated, I thought, and read the paragraph headed Treatment:

The general treatment is the same as in severe cases of lobar pneumonia due to pneumococcus.

There, I thought, it's all right, but my eyes went on skimming and I read:

. . . penicillin is not effective.

I read the whole thing again. Five days. A fulminating course of five days. And after five days? What then? In my ears I heard my own heart, each beat heavy, slow, like blows from a sadist's fist.

My father was silent on the way home. As soon as we were in the living room and without taking off his coat or hat, he went to the telephone. It was suppertime in California.

What's that? my father kept shouting. Sylvia, can't you keep those children quiet?

When it was settled, my father hung up the telephone. Yes, she would come. It would be hard to get seats, because of the Christmas traffic, but as soon as she could get them all on a plane. He walked slowly to the dining room and took off his hat and let it drop on the table. The round, globed light above the table made a white spot like a moon on the wood. My father lightly flicked his hat and the hat rocked on its battered brim, a tub anchored in moonlight. Long after I'd gone to bed, I heard him pottering in the kitchen, and the clink of his spoon as he slowly stirred cup after cup of tea.

13

When we were children, Louis, Sully and I, my mother used to fuss about Christmas, and even these last few years everything was done twice as carefully. The windows were made to sparkle, the floors gleamed, the whole house exuded a wealth of smells which rose and fell from room to room: lemon oil, pine bough, beeswax in the living room, bright tangerine smell in the kitchen, and from a hiding place in the dining room sideboard dark aromatic whiffs of the German spice cookies that came in a tin from New York.

This year when the tin arrived I did not open it. All I tried to do was to keep the house neat. Mornings I dusted and used the carpet sweeper and began to wonder what my mother had found to keep her so busy. About eleven I cooked my father's rice, and after lunch—chicken noodle or tomato soup—I read until four or five, then walked along the gray river watching chunks of ice bob and pitch. At this hour the hills across the river were always a sea-shell pink, and when they had turned quite purple I went to see my mother. There in the hospital room it was always the same sort of twilight—the ceiling globe painted everything in degrees of yellow. Nurses came and went, time passed and did not go anywhere. My mother went from wakefulness to sleep and there was no real division between the two. There had been no crisis. Her condition was about the same.

During that week my father was silent and spent much time at the hospital or in his office. He saw his occasional patients and appeared at odd times to eat the cold rice I had learned not to burn. Christmas, a Thursday, came and we ignored it. On Saturday, when I went in to see my mother, she said to me, "Please put some water in my roses, nurse," and I went home. Stephen was coming for me at seven. We were going to a party.

Waiting for the evening I felt listless and dull. The house was quiet, with a kind of lurking passivity. Cleaning it that week I had had the feeling it disliked me. It belonged to my mother. I went to the window and looked out. From this window, the center one of the bow, she had looked down into the town, and almost every evening that I had been out I had, before going in, looked up to see if her dark shape was there. Now, staring down, I saw the town with my mother's eyes. The sky was limp, not with snow but with smog, on the window sill lay a pox of soot. I pressed my cheek against the cold glass, the way I'd done when I was a careless child. If my mother should die? Through the glass came the town's own smell, a rank, sulphurous odor, the smell of the creek that, this week, the mill's dumped dyes had stained a Christmas red. At seven, when the shelf clock struck, I went into the bedroom to dress, and a little later the doorbell rang. I put on my coat and scarf and went down to meet him.

"Hi," he said, grinning and holding the door open for me. He had on the good dark suit, but over it a too-short, bright-blue topcoat. His ears, pink-rimmed, stood out as if in protest to the brittle cold.

"You wrapped up good?" he asked as we walked to the car. "The heater's conking again."

"Aren't we just going to the Ritchie's?"

"Now? Hell, it's only seven. Things won't start until nine. You want to go somewhere special first?" We got into the car—it was cold but windproof—and he asked me again if there were somewhere special I wanted to go. I couldn't think of any place. "Then let's not," he said. "We'll ride around. What do you know, for once we've got enough gas."

"It's cold to ride around," I said.

"I've got all sorts of heating equipment," he said, and turned to me and smiled. He laid his arm across the back of the seat, then dropped his fingers just inside my coat collar.

I pulled away. "You're cold."

He shrugged and started the car. I sat back and let the city glide by. In the afternoon it had snowed briefly, then melted. Now a black glaze of ice coated the streets.

"What'd you do while I was away?" he asked.

"Nothing," I said.

"Come on, the whole week? You go out with John Ritchie?"

"No," I said.

"Pete Reilly?"

"No," I said.

"Walter Ferguson?"

"My mother's been sick. She's been in the hospital."

"No kidding. My God, what's she got?"

"Pneumonia."

"When'd she get sick?"

"The Sunday you went away. Last Sunday."

"Is she all right now?"

"Yes," I said.

"Oh," he said, "that's good."

He drove out of town, going very slowly because the streets were so dark and slick. He went west for a few miles, then turned north and nosed the car back townward, but still going north, zigzagging up the hills, taking a route of gentler inclines.

"So what else'd you do?" he asked, sitting up very straight and squinting forward into the dark.

"I read."

"All the time?"

"Yes."

"What did you read?"

I told him and he laughed.

"Sounds dull," he said.

"And safe. No girl was ever raped by a book."

He laughed again, but oddly, surprised, I guess, because of what I'd said. "That's my Ellie," he said. "You want to know what I did?"

"You worked in your uncle's liquor store."

"Sure. Know what else I did?"

"No."

"I made a good bet. Hiahleah. I played Hookey Boy to place on a ten-dollar ticket. Odds were fifteen to one to win. How much do you think I made?"

"I don't know."

"Ninety-eight-twenty. Pretty good, huh?"

"You could have made more on a win ticket."

"I never bet to win."

"I know it."

"So what's wrong with ninety-eight-twenty?"

"Nothing. Now you're rich."

"Sure," he said. "Outside of that, I didn't do much. My uncle's a real Polack screw. Know what he paid me, the bastard? Fifty cents an hour. It's in the family, he says. Shit, I told him."

The road we were at last turning onto was the road that ran along the bottom of High School Hill. It was, on this vacation night, poorly sanded, and as we made the turn the tail of the car flipped dangerously. He let it unwind without braking and we rocked to a stop twenty dark yards from the street lamp. The view below was beautiful, loops and lines of lights crisscrossing and doubling back like an astronomer's map of the heavens. Since September we had been here often because of this view, although the town police, maliciously and with perverted pleasure, patrolled the street, fixing their brights on the eyes of startled lovers. This had happened to us once. Stephen, to protect me, had turned his head directly to their lights so that they would not see my frightened face.

"It sure is pretty," he said, then leaned his head back

against the seat and closed his eyes. "Damn it, I'm tired. I was so edgy last night about tonight I couldn't sleep."

"Why?" I asked. He felt under his coat for cigarettes, brought one out and lit it. His face, bent briefly over the cupped flame, was long, yellow and wan, like a tired priest's.

"I don't know. Waiting to see you, I guess. I thought while I was away maybe you'd go out with somebody else. I don't know why. Do you want a drink?" Without waiting for me to answer he reached over to the back seat and brought up a fuzzy plaid blanket and a bottle. He tucked the blanket all around us but kept an arm out to manage the bottle. This he did neatly, unscrewing the cap with one hand, then holding the bottle for me. I took a drink and tried not to choke.

"Good, huh?" he said. "It's a good Scotch. All of my last day's pay. More?" He held up the bottle again and I took another swallow.

"Hey," he said. "Enough. You might get sick." He put the bottle next to him on the seat, then cranked the window down just enough to push out his cigarette. He sighed and brought his arm carefully inside the blanket.

"It's funny," he said, "the time I spent there with my aunt and uncle—I really missed you. They've got this house, nothing fancy, but nice, pink, and new, and a coupla trees out front and my Aunt Betty keeps it neat as a pin. They've got four kids. My cousin Al's the oldest—he's nine—and the little one's name is Carrie, I like that for a girl's name, it's not Caroline or anything, just Carrie, and the kids are nice. Noisy, but nice kids. Anyway, I'd come home with Joe pretty late, because the store closed late on account of Christmas, and Betty'd have our dinner, spaghetti, or pork chops, or chicken—she's a good cook, too—then we'd watch the TV and have a coupla beers or play cards. But the funny thing was, I'd be so lonely. I'd be sitting there with them and feel lonely and you know what I'd wish? That it was our house and that you were there. Then I'd sit there watching TV and think about you and what were you doing and were you out with somebody or having a good time and it'd end up, I'd sneak out to the kitchen where they had an extension, and I'd call you. Well, geez, I called two-three nights and never got an answer. So then I really started to sweat and I couldn't sit there like that, so I went to the movies a coupla nights and played some pool. I guess you were at the hospital. But, hell, it made me mad missing you like that. Missing you so much, as if I had a big hole in my gut." He leaned against me. His hands covered mine, his strong breath warmed my cheek. His lips blew lightly near my ear, then slid across my face and toward my mouth.

"We ought to go," I said. I turned my head away. There, out the window, the view hung like a mirage—on this high ledge of a road we hung suspended between the sky and the town. Above us was nothing but speckled space, below us Clifton stretched, spangled, waiting, a netful of fallen stars.

He kissed my neck and then, again, my mouth. His hands, warm now and supple, slid up inside my coat. He kissed me, his fingers meanwhile turning the buttons of my dress. Don't, I said, and clutched his wrists, but his hands were tense with strength and his arms like rods. Don't, I said, it's too cold, but he whispered that he would warm me and his hands slid next to my skin and every bit of him felt tight, energy coiled and waiting, and his knees shoved sharply against mine. I tilted under him, pinned by his surging weight, and I struggled but his hands held me and covered my breasts. Then I lay still. He sighed. His hand slipped slowly up my thigh. I raised my arm up as if to stroke him and then hit him as hard as I could with my fist.

"Jesus," he gasped and sat up slowly, with a hand to his eye and the blanket slipping off his back. I sat up and pulled my clothes together and put my hand on the door.

"Shall I walk?"

"Ellie."

"What?"

"What's wrong?"

"Nothing."

"I wouldn't have hurt you. I wouldn't have let anything happen."

"Anything what happen?"

"A baby or anything."

"Thanks, but isn't that against your religion?"

"What?"

"Those things you carry. I wouldn't want to make you use them and sin."

He looked out of the window. "You think I wouldn't marry you?"

"Marry me?" And then I laughed. "My God, I

wouldn't marry *you*." All the way down in the valley a train whistle blew, and it came up over the top of the hill, skimming the frozen air, piercing the skin of the night, and I wondered why, after all those long brown swallows of Scotch, my head felt so clear. Words, cold and separate as tracks, hung in my head. Saying them my voice sounded hard, as if it were my mother's. "It amazes me, really, how little you know about me. You don't know at all what I'm like. I'm only a sex to you, a piece of girl. And sex is all we've ever had."

I waited for him to deny it, but instead he gathered the fallen blanket together and tossed it into the back. He started the car with a roar and we shot down the steep icy streets, skidding all the way. At my door we stopped all at once. I opened the door and got out.

"You know what?" he said before I closed it.

"What?" I asked tiredly.

"I'm sorry I didn't fuck you," he said. I carefully closed the door. The car jerked forward, its whale tail skidding sideways toward the Y, and then it straightened and went on down the street.

Upstairs, I found my father sitting in the dark, waiting for me. When I snapped on the light he blinked and looked at the clock.

"Why, it's only nine," he said.

"I was tired," I said and kicked off one shoe. My father had gotten up and was coming over to me. Before I knew why, he had reached up—in heels I was taller than he—and put his arm around me shakily and kissed me—a kiss like a timid blow—on the cheek. Then he let me go. He took off his glasses and began searching his pants pockets for something to wipe them with.

"Your mother's all right," he said, "the fever's gone down." He turned from me, and instead of wiping his glasses, vigorously blew his nose. Then he wiped the glasses on the slim, unused margin of handkerchief and readjusted them carefully, one earpiece at a time, over his ears. "It was close, very close, but she'll be home soon. When Sully comes. And we'll have to take very good care of her." We went into the kitchen and I made him a cup of tea. Over it, he told me again all the stories I had heard before, how he had met my mother at Schlegel's, and how sitting there at the cash register she never looked up, and how after going to see her up at the sanitorium he had spent the next week living on cold canned hash. When I went to bed at twelve I felt a dull ache in my body as if it were catching cold.

14

"So she's really all right?" Sully asked my father, but turned to look at me, sitting behind her in the rear seat of the car.

"Yes, all right," my father answered, "but still pretty weak. We've got to be careful not to tire her. Just be with her a half hour or so at a time. There's the new bank building, Sylvia, to your right. Hardly an improvement, would you say?"

Sully turned to observe the dun marble skin of the bank building, which had, in the year past, been newly grafted. This was the only major Clifton change we found it necessary to point out. Sully's daughter, Pam, aged two, stood pressed against my left knee and watched me closely out of her mother's eyes. Billy, the three-year-old, relentlessly maneuvered the ashtray which was built into the arm of the seat, and looked up now and then with a blue-eyed stare.

The third baby rode up front under Sully's coat, still *in utero* but six months from seed. My sister's pregnancy made her look pathetic. Appearing at the top of the train steps and looking out over the station yard for us, she had been my idea of an Okie. She wore a blue, kinky-curled coat that hung straight down, buttonless, exposing her convex middle from neck to hem. She wore thick stockings of a leather-looking brown and scratched maroon loafers; her hair was combed into a stringy chignon that was slept-on and child-pulled. Now she nervously fingered the straggles that looped at the nape of her neck. I wanted to tuck them up for her, get her into new shoes and stockings and a coat. Anything to make her seem less frowsy. Seeing her this way, I knew my mother would cry.

And she did. Propped up in her bed on three pillows, with a green V-necked sweater pulled over her pajamas, she lifted her arms to Sully and wrapped her in them, and cried. From behind their mother's bulk Sully's children looked on in awe.

"Well," my father said, grinning from the doorway, "well, well, well. Frieda, I'd like you to meet your—er—grandson—William." He presented Billy and the little boy looked out not shyly but stubbornly from behind his mother's arm. "And Pamela," my father said, and the little girl was placed, thumb-sucking still, on the edge of the bed, where she ducked her head quickly into her mother's side.

"Of course they don't know me," my mother said. "It takes time to know anyone, especially an old grandmother who lives so far away. Sit down right here, Sylvia, next to me. Was your trip terrible or nice? Oh, how wonderful you could come. Why don't you ever write? Don't we have anything for the children to play with, Eleanor? I should have thought."

I went to my mother's closet. There, on the second shelf, behind the square purple hatbox, she had always hidden birthday and Christmas presents. Now I distributed the things I had bought that morning, a rag doll for my niece, a dump truck for my nephew, some colored blocks, and two large plastic whistles. My mother still held Sully's hand and was watching the children open their things. My father leaned against the bureau and frowned, as if there were something he should be attending to. He took his watch out of his vest pocket and looked at it.

"Aha!" he said. "Four o'clock. It's time for your medicine, Frieda."

I got up to make some coffee and get the children chocolate milk, and my father came trotting out behind me. My mother said in a loud voice:

"You see, Sylvia? You see how it is? He's mad with delight, after all these years I'm in his power at last. Eleanor," she called, and I turned, letting my father march past me toward his trove of tinkling, brown-bottled medicaments. "Do you know where the album is?" she asked. "At the bottom of the sideboard, under all the table linens?"

And so with coffee and cake, chocolate for us and plain pound for my father, I served up the green album. The book was old, at least half full of starched ancestors preserved in tones of brown. As soon as my mother began turning pages, Pammy climbed up on the bed. She stood for a minute on my mother's pillow and then sat, plop, and began prodding curiously at my mother's face and at the eyeglasses she had just put on. Then Pammy stood again, but unsteadily so that my mother tried to help hold her by putting an arm aound her fat legs and with the other hand turned the crusted pages of the album. Sully called Pammy softly to her, but my mother tightened her grip and said,

"No, now, Sylvia, let her alone. She's got to get a good look at her grandmother."

My father arrived with his array of bottles and gravely lined them up on the bureau. I gave Sully coffee and cake and tried to give the children chocolate milk. Now Billy was on the other side of my mother looking at the photographs and asking "Who's 'at?" In his vigor, he skinned a snapshot off the page and sent it drifting over the edge of the bed.

"Billy," Sully said.

"Now, let him alone," my mother said. "The poor boy's been cooped up for hours traveling." Sully sighed. In her search my mother was beginning to reach modern times; pictures of us as children emerged. There was Sully in a frilly sundress, posed holding a watering can over me, a bare, angry baby.

"Look, Sylvia," my mother said, "here it is, a picture of your brother Louis when he was three. He couldn't have looked more like Billy, or Billy like him. Do you see what I mean? That expression, and the way his hair falls in his eyes."

My father, who was shaking pills out into his hand, turned to look at my mother. "It's hard to tell anything from pictures, Frieda, you know that."

"I guess he does sort of look like this picture," Sully said, bending to look. "You know, I guess it's true, Billy doesn't really look like big Bill, but I never could quite figure out . . ." She stopped and started again. "He has your eyes, though, Mother, and I guess Louis did too."

My father came over to the bed, cleared his throat loudly,

and then, with a kind of grin, handed my mother the pills. She sighed and put them all into her mouth at once, then gulped from the water glass at her bedside table. "You're delighted to be able to torture me this way," she said to my father. He was watching Billy and laughed, suddenly.

"Frieda," he said, "do you remember the time Louis was a little tyke, Billy's age I'd say. He climbed up on a chair and put his baby chair on top of that and got down a carload of my medicines."

"Oh," my mother said, "he was older than Billy, five or six." Then she laughed. "He put them in his own little play doctor's kit and went out on the street and tried to give them to passers-by. How we scolded him!"

"And what," my father asked, "was the name of that song he used to sing?"

"What song?" my mother said. "They all knew dozens of songs."

"No, I remember this one in particular," my father insisted. "Dee-da-dee-da-dum," he rumbled and looked up at the ceiling trying to conjure it. "Something about a trolley, a nickel for the trolley, and the fair." He went back to the bureau and began to collect his bottles and then, tapping his fingers, tried to summon it from the wood.

"Vaguely, vaguely, vaguely," my mother said. She laughed and pulled Pamela's hand out of her hair. "Oh, child, you're giving this old head a real massage."

My father persisted. "Da-dee-da-dee." The coffee was drunk, the chocolate milk half spilled, half downed, then my father pulled out his watch. It was four-thirty, he announced, and visiting hours were over. He stuffed his bottles into his coat pockets and went out to the kitchen. The toys were collected, and the children shushed and taken away. My mother lay back on her pillows with her eyes shut and I began quietly to put the coffee things together on the tray. The dim pink light that came in through the windows fell softly on her face, warming it into a younger color. Her hands still covered the green cloth of the album and the plain, heavy gold wedding band winked at the waist of her finger. I had lifted the tray and was walking toward the kitchen with it when the doorbell rang. As if this was the signal my pulse had settled for, it began to thud, then hammer. So he had come after all, despite everything I'd said. Footsteps came heavily up the stairs and my father shouted down, "Hello?"

"It's just Ed Schaeffer, Dr. Munson," I heard the man say. My mother's eyes flew open. There was something exposed about her expression, her eyes confused and non-public, as if shades had been sprung up on rooms too early in the day. I heard my father say something and Schaeffer said something and then my mother struggled up in bed and called out in a strained voice, "Ed? Mr. Schaeffer? Come in, come in, I'm wide awake." I picked up the tray and went into the kitchen. Over my shoulder I saw Schaeffer coming down the hall dangling a bunch of red roses and behind him, guarding him well, my frowning father, and chugging behind my father, his friend Pamela, who was trailing behind her the yellow, yarn-haired doll.

"Daddy," I yelled, putting my tray down. "You go on

with Pamela. I'll bring Mr. Schaeffer some coffee." My father hesitated, then in a defensive sweep swung up the little girl and carried her and the doll back toward the living room, where soon it began to sound like the circus, with the children screaming and my father growling and roaring and Sully alternately cajoling and threatening and laughing. I warmed up the coffee slowly; it was, after all, quite cold, and I warmed it up again, slowly, then poured it, steaming, into a cup, and cut, carefully and slowly, a large piece of the chocolate cake, and slowly and carefully took this back to the bedroom.

"Oh!" I said at the doorsill, pretending to trip a little. They sat without a light in the rose-and-plum-colored last of the sunset. Schaeffer sat on the straight chair next to my mother's bed. He had not taken off his coat, and with his head hung down and the roses drooping between his hands, was studying the floor space between his knees. My mother looked up at me slowly with strange eyes which, in the deep-colored almost-dark, seemed blank and colorless as mirrors.

"Turn on the light, please, Eleanor," she said. I put the coffee and cake down and turned on a small lamp. The light in the room was suddenly a golden coffee color and Schaeffer looked up.

"Oh, El'ner," he said. "You didn't fix that all for me, did you?"

"I thought I'd trade you the flowers for the coffee."

He looked dumbly at the roses he held. "I almost did forget them."

"More roses, Ed," my mother said. "You're really too

extravagant. The last ones were so beautiful. You know, all the time I lay asleep in the hospital, I dreamed of the smell of roses. I dreamed the same dream over and over—I was a child again and it was summer. I was very young, four or five, and my family lived in Koppelshaven. My mother was still alive. I thought I was in her garden and she was cutting roses. The sky was a wonderful blue and the air so clean. Just down through the village was the beach—beautiful white sand, very white—and then the sea. It's always seemed to me, in memory anyway, that the Baltic is one of the most beautiful bodies of water. I don't suppose you've been there?"

"No. No, I've never traveled out of New York State."

"I'd like to go to Germany some day. Despite all that's happened. I'd like to see the place where my mother is buried. And my son."

There was a silence and I said, "Why don't you try the coffee, Mr. Schaeffer? I thought it was good."

"Oh, it is good," he agreed hastily. "Very good."

"It's instant," I said, "but I make it up a quart at a time. I think that improves the flavor."

"Wonderfully," my mother said, and laughed.

"I don't understand how to work your coffee pot," I said.

My mother smiled and shook her head; Mr. Schaeffer gulped his coffee. He ate the cake in two great bites, then stood up, still chewing, and brushing cake crumbs from his coat.

"Well, Frieda," he said, turning to my mother, "best of

luck to you. I'm real glad to hear you're on the road to health again. If you ever need help—construction work of any kind—I'll be right there."

My mother held out her hand and thanked him. They shook hands. I saw him out to the door. He waved good-bye to Sully and to my father, still down on his knees with the children, and then went down the stairs in his gangling, stiff-kneed way, and went out the inner and then the outer door. I went back to my mother's room to put the roses in water. She had turned on her side and appeared to be asleep. I took the album from the bed and put it on the chair, then took the roses and left the room

Sully cooked dinner while I observed. It was, as my father said, the first edible meal we'd had in ten days. She'd brought Christmas presents with her in her luggage, a Waring blender for my mother which pulverized a whole dinner for my father in no time at all. He was amazed. After dinner we bedded the children down toe to toe on the living-room sofa. My father disappeared, humming, to his office. Sully and I did the dishes. With the kinky blue coat off and her hair neatly redone she looked less like a document out of the nineteen-thirties. The stockings, she told me, were rubber, for her bad legs; and because her legs were tired she sat down next to the sink and dried the dishes I washed. We caught up on each other. They had their own house, "little but cute," and the flowers grew down the back slope like weeds. Bill liked his job in the airplane plant and was still taking courses at night. And how was I? Was I going out?

"Out?" I said. "How do you mean?"

"You know how I mean," she said, smiling at me.

I shrugged. I had been, I said, but we had had a fight and I wouldn't be going out with him anymore.

"Oh, Bill and I had a million fights," she said. "Is he nice?"

I said that, well, yes, he was nice, but I didn't want to go out with him all the time. I didn't want to get involved.

"Well," Sully said, "you're right. Don't get stuck." She finished drying the cup she was working on and put it on its saucer. "What I mean is, don't get married too young. I know you're going to think now I don't love Bill, but that's not true. We're not even tired of each other yet. My gosh, he's not home that much. That's the trouble. It's just me and the kids, me and the kids, all the time. Working and going to school nights, he's just home weekends. Then everything's fine and I feel so good I do all kinds of extra things, make cupcakes and bake pies. But when he's not home I'm all by myself, and we live pretty far out, and to save money for the new baby we can't afford to get another car and I can't get anywhere. I'm home all the time. Sometimes it's like a jail, that house." I looked at her, and there she was, just the way she used to be, examining the hangnail on her thumb with that pouty look on her face, and I thought to myself, I wonder what it would take to make her happy. It depressed me that she was so unhappy, just the way she used to be at home. And then she sighed and got up and began putting the china away. Well, I thought, all she ever wanted was the Big Trap and now she's in it and hates it. I let the water out of the sink and scoured the sink with cleanser. But not for me, I thought. I don't want it. Wasting my time waiting on some idiot man and his sticky kids. When there are so many better things to do. And I rinsed the dishcloth out in extra-hot water and spread it on the counter to dry.

At nine o'clock I went in to give my mother her last medicine of the night. With the pills I took in the crystal vase full of roses. I set them down on the dresser where they nodded and swayed against their reflections in the mirror. My mother woke up and looked up at them.

"Mr. Schaeffer is the nicest man," I said.

"Yes," she said.

"He came to see you several times while you were in the hospital. Did Daddy tell you?"

"Did he? No, he didn't." She sat up and began to peel the covers from her legs. A noise in the pipes made her stop. "Well, now I *know* Sylvia's home," she said, "*and* in the bathroom."

I brought my mother the medicines. She took them from my cupped hand, swallowed them straight down without water.

"My poor Sylvia. Did you see the way she looked? She's a wreck, a frump, and she was so beautiful. Nothing fades beauty faster than child-bearing. She'll be worn out before she's twenty-five. What's the matter with her legs? Veins? Where'd she get that, I wonder. I never had anything like that. Oh, but they're wonderful children, aren't they, Eleanor? Little Billy's so bright, you can tell that *immediately*. And Pammy's so lovable. It's been years since I held a child. Funny, you forget how they feel, their wonderful skin, so soft, and the lovely spongy feel of their fat. Mmm. Couldn't you just squeeze them? That little laugh of Pammy's—heh, heh. They're beautiful, yes, they are. Did you talk to Sylvia at all? Does she seem happy?"

"You know Sully," I said, "but she's happy enough. They have a nice little house and a garden. Bill's earning lots of money and going to school so that he can earn more."

"Well," my mother said, "that's nice. Comfort is all I've ever asked for Sylvia." She sighed. "It was nice to see your father enjoy his grandchildren. Do they seem to like him?" I said I thought they did. "I'm glad," she said. "These last years haven't been very happy for him. He needs a little happiness. I know it's been hard on you sometimes, Eleanor. I mean the fact that your father has—peculiarities. But at least they're not vices. I've always been grateful that he didn't drink. Oh, he always was a strange man. He knew more about things and less about people than anyone I'd ever met. Louis was the one who kept him on even keel. He got through to him, I don't know how. *I* never learned. Still, he's a good man at heart. I don't know what he'd do without me. He's never even learned to make tea. Nearly thirty years that we've been married. What an investment that is. What sheer bulk of time."

The pipes yowled suddenly and through the wall we heard water rushing downward. "At last," my mother said.

She edged her legs over the bed, then stood up, leaning heavily on me. We walked slowly to the bathroom. Sully came out in a quilted blue silk robe, looking pink and scrubbed, my teen-age sister again.

"The baby's really kicking tonight," she said. She put her hand on it and smiled passing us.

I helped my mother to the toilet. She stood there supporting herself with a hand on the top of the tank. "No," she said to me, "don't ever give up your memories. Not at my age, anyway, because it's most of what you'll have." And she dismissed me with a wave of her hand.

PART III

Memories indeed, when what I'd fed on were fat hopes.

At college my room was a corner room, draughty but pleasant, and when it was windy maple branches knocked against the panes. For the first two years I had a roommate, but we parted amicably, eremites dedicated to art and history. Memories! The whole history of mankind was what I wanted to learn. The room had aqua wallpaper and I made a bedspread out of red bark-cloth. The curtains were thick and shaggy, oatmeal textured. I kept the room neat, liking a slightly barren look to my belongings, but books overflowed and had to be stacked against the walls. Black books predominated. Thick, unwieldy black-bound volumes of the *Economic History Review;* black also for Bishop Stubbs and Otto of Freising. Copies of *Speculum* were sky-blue, books in the Berkshire series navy. I do not remembre what color Pirenne was. Red or blue, which was it? I found him, hard cover, in a Marboro bookstore on 42nd Street, one day during a spring vacation. At nineteen I loved him, for his vast imagination romped across all of Europe, went east, drew into one net Byzantium, the Goths, Mecca, Rome. From heaped erudition he tossed out facts like coins to beggars, and these struck sparks that suddenly lit up for me the rough faces of those centuries. At nineteen I wanted more than anything else to be a great medievalist.

But I was greedy. There were other things to read. I made lists of what I would learn when I got out of college and my time was my own. I wanted to study art, music, philosophy, and languages, particularly Russian, Greek, and Italian. I wanted to learn something about physics. My ignorance exhausted me; the more I learned the less I saw I knew. Chasing elusive knowledge I was drawn onto strange terrain, into cold countries I did not know, where plains extended for miles behind me, and looking up I saw nothing but brown plains ahead. In the middle of my senior year in college my mother wrote that Stephen had had a third child.

Often that last year in high school I saw his ice-cold head moving down the hall in front of me, but we never spoke, not even to say hello or good-bye. It was a tense year for me, dedicated to making a college. For comic relief I went out with John Ritchie. He took me to lavish places, the Kokomo Club near Albany and a place outside of Saratoga Springs where we spent several evenings eating seafood in crimson splendor. Afterward we necked in his fancy wine-red Triumph. The car's upholstery was slick, red and black, and everything, windows, lighter, descending top, worked in smooth clicks and springs. But it was not a good car for necking; sitting sunk so far down in its pitlike belly I had an uncomfortable sense of sin. After an evening with him I went home feeling tough as a middle-aged whore. I would lock myself into the bathroom and stare into the mirror, then claw hatefully at a pimple on my chin. As if by thus disfiguring my face I could avenge myself on him for kissing me. I went out with him because he was going to Yale. He pleased my mother because she saw I hated him.

And Stephen? He took out Rosalind Marsh, a girl always strictly for laughs, with snub face and enormous breasts. Even in grammar school her name had been Cow Marsh. In class her round brown eyes were moist with boredom, she was forever hiking up her thick pink straps. But, I asked myself contemptuously, why do you care? Because, for all his brown-eyed needs, he haunted me. I caught myself saying "coulda." The smell of frying hamburgers made me ill. Sometimes, touching my body in the most matter-of-fact way, undressing or bathing, I felt it stiffen treacherously, tingle, as if there lingered in it a residual fire. Oh, the cheapness of it, I thought, loving him the way some men love great-bosomed women, for their pure dumb sex. And how I disliked this in myself.

On the day before I was married I went out to buy stockings and, desperate amateur, a cookbook. The weather was bright, if windy. Walking down Park Street toward the bookstore I swung my purse and sang the first aria from *Figaro* where Susannah and Figaro measure their room for a bed. Da-de-dum-dum-dum-dum *cin-que,* Da-de-dum-dum-dum-dum *die-ci,* and there he was. He was standing in front of a closed-down sports goods store that had hastily been turned into a state unemployment office. The Club, Clifton called it. I saw him long before he saw me. Walking toward him, I felt my legs wobble as if every joint I owned pulled separately. I went up to him and spoke. After a frozen moment he said hello. I asked him how he was and he said, uh, fine, and all the while the men he was standing with stared, coughed, turned away, examined the scraped soles of their shoes. I was very conscious of how I looked. I had on a sheer gray cotton dress that fit tight down to the hips and then was full, and because the wind that day was strong I had to stand talking to him with my arms clamped to my sides. I was conscious too of my gloves. I had a passion for short white cotton gloves and wore them even in Clifton where they were an ostentation. I asked about his children and he said they were fine, great kids. And then I blundered and said, "It's awful about the mills closing. Do you think you'll get another job soon?" His face shut up and he shrugged.

"Sure, why not? This is just temporary. A small vacation on the government. Just because they move the goddam mills doesn't mean this place'll be a ghost-town."

I nodded. "I guess there are lots of jobs in other places."

"Sure," he said. "There's nothing to worry about." I tried to smile. He offered me a cigarette and when I shook my head no, he said, "Christ, you never did know how to smoke." Then we really did smile at each other. "Hey," he said. "I guess you're getting married soon. That's what I read in the paper a coupla weeks back."

I said yes, I was. Tomorrow, in fact.

"Some rich guy, huh?"

This made me laugh. No, I said, not rich at all. And we were both going to study.

"Yeah?" he said. "Well, good luck." I wished the same to him. I put out my hand and after a moment he took it and we shook hands awkwardly, as if our palms had scorched. Then I nodded good-bye and went on down the street. All the way down the block I had to fight my skirts, knowing that the men in the Club were watching. Walking away from him I was glad that, saying good-bye, I had looked so well, and then, remembering how he looked, felt my stomach fall. His shirt was faded, the pocket half torn off, his khakis unpressed and grease-spotted at the knees. His wife, they said, was a slob. I thought how different it might have been for him and this made me angry. He was too good to toss on the compost of pure procreation. It had taken me these four years to understand what he had given me, that love was process, not entity, and that once having loved, even selfishly, I might ultimately love generously. That generated power was there. Thinking this, I saw I had passed the bookstore and had to turn back to get my cookbook. I bought not one but two, and came out of the store with a feeling of bland contentment. Food somehow made me think of love and as I went on down the street it occurred to me pleasurably that I would be married tomorrow and loved tomorrow night.

I am sitting in this little darkness waiting. Clothes timidly touch my hair. Unknown objects protrude. Outside the door—the downstairs bedroom; beyond this—tight-muscled walls; past this—rain: straight steel bars. Upstairs, over my head, the children are running, a patternless pattern like strings of beads breaking. They are in the front bedroom.

You asked me, Sully, *why*, and I didn't know what to say. I am hiding here, trying to think. I think how life goes on endlessly turning—birth to death, death to birth—how just living can grind you down small. Sometimes, passing a mirror, I see my mother's face rise up out of my bones. *Look*, you said, *look what motherhood* (that great leveler) *has done to you. What was all the fuss for?* They are coming down the stairs.

And, you said, *look at the way you live*. Meaning, how could I do without your MG, your Mexican maid, your house full of insolent gadgets. Meaning, this broken-down house furnished with children and books. For me, occasional money buys only a gift of time. In it, so much to see, hear, feel, and ponder. Your time is a cracked jug, mine a leaky boat. You must continually fill time, I empty it. Perhaps, after all, it was for this: I am never bored. I haven't acquiesced to memory. Daily the fact that I am alive unfolds in me, fresh as a flower.

235

Clattering. Doors slam, walls shake. Through the dining room, the living room, here. The dark door splits, light thunders in. Found. Clamors surround me. All right, my fat sweet brats, I'll tell you a story. Now listen. Once upon a time, in a cool green pond, lived a frog who was also a princess.

Perennial Fiction Library
Harper & Row, Publishers

World-Class Writing

Title	Price	No.
___ HAWKSMOOR by Peter Ackroyd	$7.95	09-13905
___ PITCH DARK by Renata Adler	$6.95	09-71440
___ SPEEDBOAT by Renata Adler	$7.95	09-71432
___ NOVEL WITH COCAINE by M. Ageyev	$6.95	09-70004
___ THE OLD DEVILS by Kingsley Amis	$7.95	09-71465
___ TO THE LAND OF THE CATTAILS by Aharon Appelfeld	$6.95	09-71150
___ THE PROPHETEERS by Max Apple	$7.95	09-61581
___ STARING AT THE SUN by Julian Barnes	$7.95	09-71481
___ RED SKY AT MORNING by Richard Bradford	$6.95	09-13616
___ THE MISALLIANCE by Anita Brookner	$6.95	09-71341
___ ONE WAY OR ANOTHER by Peter Cameron	$5.95	09-14218
___ BLISS by Peter Carey	$7.95	09-13558
___ ILLYWHACKER by Peter Carey	$9.95	09-13319
___ CONTINENT by Jim Crace	$6.95	09-14770
___ ALL WE NEED OF HELL by Harry Crews	$6.95	09-14606
___ BLOOD & GRITS by Harry Crews	$6.95	09-14598
___ THE GOSPEL SINGER by Harry Crews	$6.95	09-71515
___ A PERIOD OF CONFINEMENT by Moira Crone	$6.95	09-71085
___ LUISA DOMIC by George Dennison	$6.95	09-13855
___ A TALE OF PIERROT by George Dennison	$8.95	09-61698
___ THE OLD GRINGO by Carlos Fuentes	$5.95	09-70632
___ THE LOVER OF HORSES by Tess Gallagher	$6.95	09-14358
___ THE ALL OF IT by Jeannette Haien	$6.95	09-71473
___ COLLECTED STORIES by Gabriel García Márquez	$7.95	09-13061
___ FOREVER FLOWING by Vasily Grossman	$6.95	09-13178
___ LIFE AND FATE by Vasily Grossman	$10.95	09-13848
___ YELLOWFISH by John Keeble	$7.95	09-14432
___ CONFEDERATES by Thomas Keneally	$7.95	09-14465
___ LOVE OUT OF SEASON by Ella Leffland	$7.95	09-13020
___ RUMORS OF PEACE by Ella Leffland	$7.95	09-13012
___ ORSINIAN TALES by Ursula K. Le Guin	$6.95	09-14333
___ THE WIND'S TWELVE QUARTERS by Ursula K. Le Guin	$6.95	09-14341
___ A BIGAMIST'S DAUGHTER by Alice McDermott	$7.95	09-71424